ABOUT THE AUTHOR

M. L. Tompsett is an emerging contemporary romance author, and this is her seventh published book. She has been crafting worlds to escape to since she was a little girl. Years later, she continues to enjoy writing in imaginative, make-believe worlds filled with exciting characters, diverse locations, and various tropes as she ventures into the large, wide, and scary world of digital and print book publishing, including audio.

Married to her childhood sweetheart, they reside in Victoria, Australia, and have two extremely talented adult sons. M. L. Tompsett is thrilled to see something she has been creating become a reality as a published book.

When she's not typing away on her keyboard for the next page-turning novel while sipping tea and munching on licorice, she's busy working on digital files for one of her many talented clients' next book releases — or capturing random scenic photos around Australia.

Check out M. L. Tompsett on her website, blog, or social media.

www.mltompsett.com

f facebook.com/M.L.TompsettAuthor
📷 instagram.com/mltompsett.author
BB bookbub.com/profile/m-l-tompsett

ALSO BY M. L. TOMPSETT

CONTEMPORARY ROMANCE

SECOND CHANCE AT LOVE - *series*

Insta Bride

The Bodyguard's Convenient Marriage

Ghost of a Chance in Love

Secret Heiress

Paranormal Fantasy

SEX, LIES AND FAMILY SECRETS - series

The Guy Next Door - Book one

Dark Surprises - Book two

You Never Know - Book three

It's You - Book four

What You Know - Book five

OTHER VAMPIRE BOOKS

Her Vampire Fated Mate

Urban Fantasy

Shifter Romance

Kept in the Dark of Love and Lust

Kept in the Dark of Lies and Deceit - book two

Non- Fiction

My Travel Log

(Print Book Only)

Contemporary Romance

THE BODYGUARD'S CONVENIENT MARRIAGE

SECOND CHANCE AT LOVE

M. L. Tompsett

Tompsett Publishing™

For my Family.
Love you guys.

Also

To all my readers who have given me the chance to write a new genre

Thank you
♡
This is for you.

♡

*Also, while writing this book, a wonderful family friend
died of cancer.
Unfortunately, he only had a short time from diagnosis to
the day he gained his angel wings.
He will be truly missed.*

*Our hearts continue to break and weep.
Our wet tears slow and run dry.
Memories of life may come and go.
But, the memories of you shall remain and stay.*

*Miss you, Pete.
Your quick wit and talent with numbers always
amazed me.
Forever in our aching hearts and fondest memories.*

To you the reader

*Please, have a medical check-up. Have your moles and
spots checked. Have yearly blood work done. If you cough
or pass, blood, have it checked as soon as possible. If you
just don't feel right and it continues more than a few days,
and it is out of the norm for you – Don't leave it thinking
it will go away.
Go to your doctor.*
Life is far too short.

♡

BLURB

Too busy for romance. Unworthy of love.

Never one for relationships, hard-working retired-FBI agent **Essy Raiker** has made it her mission to be the best bodyguard in the business. Complete the contract. Don't get attached. Don't get hooked. Rules to live by for a kid starved of love and abandoned into foster care. That is, until the day Declyn Bianchi hired her, changing her life forever.

More than bullets fly hot and fast when Essy faces her estranged husband.

Declyn Bianchi is fed up with his high society family controlling his life and the reckless antics of his trouble-seeking identical twin. Dekk's prayers are answered in the form of a sinful-looking body—his new bodyguard, Essy Raiker.

Family is everything to Dekk. So, when their safety is threatened, he risks danger to save them. Then the family he thought he could trust betrays him, and he turns to his estranged wife for help.

Can Essy risk rejection and let Dekk in, exposing her fragile heart? Can Dekk reveal his feelings for Essy and protect his heart from breaking again?
Who is behind the attacks against the Bianchi family? And can they be stopped before everything Essy and Dekk value is lost?
Not all secrets remain dead and buried. Some lurk beneath the surface, waiting for the right moment to strike.

Passions burn deep in this second chance at love.

THE
BODYGUARD'S
CONVENIENT
MARRIAGE

Believe in yourself.
Trust your feelings.
Only you can take the next step
Life is not ending
It is just starting, to a new future.

— *M. L. Tompsett*

Chapter One

ESSY

*G*reat... nothing like going in blind when you're on a mission.

Military and FBI training only went so far. One glance around the elaborate gala venue already displays the building structure differs from the blueprints I memorized this afternoon.

Side-stepping the champagne-carrying, nose-in-the-air guests, I survey the entries and exits again. The array of guests. The multitude of potential risks and danger points. Right this minute, I'd prefer my work leathers and Glock instead of high heels and an evening gown.

Laini steps in beside me. "How in the world did you convince security to let us in?" she whispers, eagerly scanning the crowd of exquisitely dressed guests with expensive jeweled accessories worth more than a year's salary. Knowing my adopted sister and best friend, she absorbs as much detail as possible—a smorgasbord of wall-to-wall celebrities for her next front-page article.

Nervous energy fills me as I wiggle my fingers. I've

lost count of the number of times my thumb brushes the gold band on my ring finger, and my heart flutters with the memory of the man who put it there. The warm strip of intricate gold with sapphire and diamond settings—the family heirloom I vowed never to remove —was our pass to getting into the elite party, and thankfully it worked. If not, my gorgeous sister was my contingency plan. Who wouldn't allow a well-known freelance editor and reporter of one of the most glamorous international, cosmopolitan magazines into their party? The annoyingly rich and famous have hounded Laini to enhance their social status through her interviews.

All I know is that the man I am hunting should appear tonight. I have to remind myself to remain professional. At all times keep my heart and emotions under control and under wraps. And most of all, do not show any weakness. Even though I have missed him every day since we parted ways, we'd agreed to a marriage of convenience. Little does he know our well-laid-out plans have changed.

I squint towards the overhead balcony and ceiling, eyeing for threats — all clear. The only danger up there and above me is the eight large crystal chandeliers. If they don't fall and shred you to ribbons, they'll squash you like a bug. The thousands of hanging crystals might blind you, from their bright radiance reflected throughout the large room.

Where are my sunglasses when I need them?

Speakers strategically placed around the room emit an insistent thrum of pop music as it fills the air. People sway to the beat while chatting, their voices blending in a chaotic murmur. My eyes, constantly on the move, scanning the dark corners of the room, unable to shake the feeling of unease. My fingers twitch eagerly for my gun with each new hiding position.

The mental tally increases as I add three more suspicious men to my growing count. Within seconds, I have their features and details memorized.

"Essy, how long are we staying here?" Laini nags, interrupting my surveillance. "Standing in line as long as we did, my feet already hurt in these ridiculous high heels." My eyes roll at her annoying comments. If I did not love her as I do, I would up-slap her.

I rub my extended belly again, feeling movement within.

Without meaning to, I roll my eyes again and groan, "Laini..." I had previously warned her... "I said for you to wear something else." And glance down at her elegant, painted, sparkling red pretty toenails peeping out from her Jimmy Choo-Sacora heels. Shoes she tries to avoid.

Laini is more at home in a pair of flats in different colors and styles, even though the woman has a room full of shoes, different types, styles, colors, and designs. The lucky bitch receives shoes by the box full. Jealous much...you betcha ya. Well, sometimes—but I still love her with all my heart. You name it, she's probably got them. Not only designers but also different companies give her shoes, hoping she likes them enough to write about them, and wear them in public—it all comes down to advertising to these people. Seen to be admired and making sales. Lucky for me, we wear the same size shoes.

I release a sigh... If only I could see both of my feet at the same time. My pregnancy is affecting me more than I realized. Sure, I can look after myself, but I've kept a false sense of bravery long enough. I'd prefer to be pampered by a caring and loving man. I am over being by myself, and I'm lonely. My FBI and military hardcore persona can only go so far. Even though my sister can be annoying, at least I can count on her — she will always have my back, and I love her for it. Thus why she is here, standing right by my side.

With one of my gorgeous Araborda Acora Christian Louboutin poking out from beneath my gown, I barely see the tips of my scarlet red painted toenails. My hand rests on my hip, and my fingers stretch and press into my side. If I could get away with it — from Ms. Eagle Eyes beside me — I would rub the annoying niggle on my lower back. The stupid pain has been there since I woke up this morning. Instead, I keep surveying the different people, taking in their features, and assessing who might be a threat and who is not.

"Okay. But you said we're attending a fancy gala. What else was I meant to wear?" She takes a step closer and glances over my body. Then down to my gorgeous shoes. "I don't know how you can stand in those shoes with your pregnant belly." I cringe at her words. My nerves are ragged enough that I don't need my sister, making me feel inadequate. "Shouldn't you be lying down instead of standing on your feet?" Whoa. Low blow.

My attempt at biting my tongue from snapping at the woman fails. "Quit it, Laini," I growl from the side of my mouth. "I'm pregnant, not an invalid." I automatically place my hand on my belly and continue glancing over at the guests, taking a deep breath. "Now, shhh. I've said we are here to find someone," I hiss as I glance over to the left side of the room, noting the different guests.

My hand gently strokes the side of my belly. Pressure beneath my hand increases, and I feel my babe's back curve before they turn and roll into another position while practicing their karate moves. Just like their father — impatient — and I continue to rub and soothe my belly.

Soon, little one. We will see your daddy... soon.

"Geez. Don't mind me if I care," Laini murmurs under her breath. I swivel to retort back when something causes me to pause. That look in her eyes. It finally occurs to me. Since she arrived this morning, sadness has filled her. Her radiant, happy self has basically vanished. Laini usually comes back from Australia in a joyous mood. All smiles. Something has placed sadness in her eyes. Before the night is out, I will make sure she reveals whatever has made her sad, and I'll place a smile back on her gorgeous face.

When Laini's eyes widen, I turn and follow her stare. The handsome man I am hunting is on the other side of the room — my MIA husband. My teeth grind together when I see his arm draped around a beautiful blonde-haired woman.

What the hell?

If I was not pregnant, I would march right up to the playboy and punch him in the nose before sending him to the ground with bruised balls.

Nah, I think I might just do it anyway and smile at my thoughts.

When I hear Laini pant, I come back to reality. "Oh, my. Who is that sexy specimen? I wonder if he is with that bimbo."

I tilt my chin and glare at the man. "I don't know," I say a little too forcefully, "but I'm going to find out."

With my feet already in motion, warmth surrounds my arm, causing me to halt. I glance down and see Laini's fingers around my forearm. "Hey. I was only joking," she squeaks. "That guy is out of my league." Why does she do that to herself? My gorgeous sister is better than all the rich women here. She has to stop putting herself down. With a lift of her chin, she meets my eyes. "And your pregnancy hormones are turning you into a bitch." Ouch...I just about feel bad for the way I have acted tonight. Although I wouldn't agree completely, my pregnancy hormones are not entirely to blame. "Come on, Essy. There is no one of interest to interview here. Let's leave before they hound me or kick us out."

My shoulders slump, and I sigh. "Laini, let go of my arm. I know that man."

Chapter Two

ESSY

"*H*uh. How do you know him?" Laini mutters as she finally lets go of my arm.

I surge forward before she can grab me again, dodging people left and right, eyes locked on my target.

"Wait for me, Essy," she hisses. "Slow down, will ya." She's already huffing. "For a pregnant woman, you sure can move fast."

Slow down? Not happening. I wasn't top of my FBI class for nothing. I'm here for one reason: to figure out why my so-called playboy husband has basically vanished. M.I.A. Ignored my calls. Ghosted my messages. Should I keep going?

It's been over four months since my FBI assignment ended, and our communication has shriveled from rare texts to nothing. Weeks since the last weird message, and then his number just...poof, disconnected. Being ghosted is a brand-new experience for me, and spoiler alert: I hate it. Time for a face-to-face.

The man in question laughs at something a

gorgeous redhead says. The blonde glued to his side slithers closer, frowning. Geez. Any closer and she'll be wearing him like a second skin. The redhead drifts off, but his eyes stay glued to her butt. Typical male. One-track mind.

My shoulders sag. Pride kept me from telling him how I really felt, and now it might be too late. If he's acting like a slime ball, I don't want him anyway. Trust has always been my Achilles' heel, thanks to foster care days. I stare at his smile, and my heart cracks a little more. So much for finding someone I could trust.

Not now, Essy. Quit the pity party.

I lift my chin, eye him, and huff. Marriage of convenience or not, cheating is not part of the deal — especially when I'm carrying his child. Correction: children.

My security instincts kick in. Where the hell are his bodyguards? I thought I trained him better.

Annoyance spikes. His bodyguards should be glued to him. Either he ignored my advice again, or something's wrong.

Each step closer, the foreboding crawls up my spine. I scan left, right, searching for threats. Nothing. Still, something feels off.

Then I zero in on the blonde clamped to his arm.

The ache in my chest sharpens. She's stunning. I'm out of my league. No wonder he ghosted me.

My FBI instincts scream at me: Look closer. Compare.

Why the hell would I compare myself to Blondie Barbie?

I swallow my pride and scan her head to toe. Fake smile, teeth too white to be real, eyes colder than a tax audit. Bottle-blonde hair, knock-off Louboutins. At least I'm real — head to toe, shoes included. And yet my so-called husband stands there grinning with her plastered to his side.

Finally, he notices me. His smile fades as his eyes sweep over my very pregnant body.

He slips away from her and steps forward. His hands touch me — and what the hell? This man is not my husband.

I meet his gaze, recognition slamming into me before he pulls me into an embrace.

"Hello, Sweets. What are you doing here?" Leo'ando whispers, voice dripping sensuality.

Monkey hairy balls. He might be Declyn's identical twin, but dammit, I want my husband, not his copy.

I breathe slow, lean in. "Heya, Leo. Looking good as ever," I whisper, arms wrapping around him. "I'm wondering where my husband is." My voice is sharp enough to cut glass. Just then, my baby kicks against him.

"Whoa. What the...?" Leo steps back, eyes dropping to my bulge.

He presses his hand where the baby kicked. The little one moves again, and his face lights up. "Wow. This kid likes me."

No. This kid is smart enough not to trust his uncle.

Leo looks up, smile fading when he sees my glare. Brow arched, I wait.

"Ahh. Essy, my beautiful one, we need to talk."

No shit, Sherlock. My eyes narrow. "Damn right, we need to talk."

The blonde swoops in, hand on his chest, flashing a diamond ring so massive it could double as a weapon. Fourteen carats, easy. Hope she doesn't swim with it — she'll sink straight to the bottom. Claim staked. Fine. She can have him.

She notices Laini at my side, and her fake smile widens like she's just spotted Santa. My sister, ever the genius, turns her head, pretending to be fascinated by another guest.

Not today, Blondie.

Sometimes Laini cracks me up. Instead of laughing, I refocus on Leo — whose lust-filled eyes are glued to my breasts, framed perfectly by my silver-white gown.

Eww. And seriously, buddy? Eyes up here.

"Darling...who is your little friend?" the beauty says through clenched teeth. Wow. Blondie has officially given up on Laini and zeroed back in on Leo. His eyes widen at her words. From the look on his face, he's completely forgotten the woman glued to his side. Typical Leo — attention span of a goldfish.

From the sparkly rock on her finger, I wonder if Leo has gotten himself a fiancée. Maybe hell has frozen over. Then again, the weather has turned bitterly cold lately, so maybe that tracks.

The strange thing is, Leo never forgets when he has a beautiful woman hanging off him — so something's up. Who is this woman, and what does she mean to him?

My thoughts flicker back to when I finished my

contract months ago with Declyn, followed by that weekend of surprises with both Dekk and Leo. A once-in-a-lifetime event — emphasis on the "never to be repeated" part. Then the next day, our small wedding ceremony, tropical getaway, and Dekk urging me never to remove his family ring from my finger — before I left him for the FBI assignment.

I place my hand on my prominent bulge and rub gently against the babe moving inside.

The blonde beauty notices my hand. Well, the ring. Her eyes widen, mouth forming a perfect O. She glances up, meeting my eyes with an angry scowl. Oh, here we go — Blondie Barbie doesn't like competition.

With an internal headshake at her attitude, I glance back at Leo, brow raised high.

"Babe, I think introductions are in order, don't you?" I murmur, dripping sarcasm. Leo hates being called Babe. Which is exactly why I say it. Inside, I'm laughing my head off.

He shakes his head, shooting me a look that screams *you'll pay for that.* Through clenched teeth, he says, "Essy, this is Caroline. Caroline, meet Essynda." His hand lands on my elbow. "Sweets. I'll escort you upstairs." He turns to Blondie and smiles. "Caroline, I have a meeting with the lovely Essynda." He lifts his wrist, Rolex flashing, cufflink sparkling like he's auditioning for a jewelry commercial.

Damn Leo. He's dodging Declyn's name like it's radioactive. Where is my husband?

Caroline scowls at Leo, then at me. Her scowl sharpens into full-blown fury as she snaps back to Leo.

"Like hell you do, Leo'ando. Who in the hell is this stranger? And whose child is she carrying?" Jealous much? Blondie's claws are out, and she's scratching at air.

My lips twitch, and I smirk. Leo's got his hands full with this aggressive Barbie doll. I turn and catch Laini's wide-eyed stare. Poor girl looks like she's watching a soap opera live.

"Come on, Laini. Leo here will escort us somewhere to sit down!" I say, voice light but loaded.

She blinks a few times, glances down at my belly, then at Leo, then back at me. Repeat. Poor thing looks like she's trying to solve a Rubik's Cube with her eyes.

"Yep. Sure," Laini murmurs. "I'm right behind you." She turns and starts walking toward the entrance we came in.

My poor sister is confused, lost, and probably regretting ever agreeing to tag along. I'll make it up to her later. Maybe with chocolate. Or wine. Or both.

Chapter Three

DEKK

The vibration of my cell alerts me to a new message.

Come on. Who the hell is messaging me now?

If I'm discovered...

Never mind those morbid thoughts. Whoever is sending me bloody texts in the middle of surveillance is going to regret it.

My brother comes to mind, reminding me I'm late for his BS engagement party. I still can't figure out what stunt Leo is pulling with that bitch Caroline.

At least this time, I know I won't be bailing him out when he gets into female or engagement trouble. I'm legally married now — to a sexy, lethal woman.

She's sensual, loyal, feisty. She put her hand up to help me when I needed her. The only thing I didn't disclose at the time was why Leo and I wanted her to join us for a night of passion. For us, it came down to a stupid family curse that's plagued the Bianchi men for centuries. Basically, a countdown to perform a secret ceremony with a willing woman… or die. Our father never explained the full story. He just encouraged us to bed someone meaningless.

Back then, I wanted Essy. And I got her. Hot-blooded male, guilty as charged — the sex was off the charts.

But I wanted more. I wanted her by my side full-time. And my gorgeous bodyguard agreed to marry me.

A smile tugs at my lips. Her full name is Essynda Raiker, Essy for short, but in my head she's Synn. Sin in nature, sin in body, sin in my bed. If she ever hears me call her that, she'll have my balls in a vice.

Synn said she avoided her adoptive parents' ridiculous wedding scheme by secretly marrying me. She was never interested in marrying for love. Her career is dangerous, takes her around the world — not exactly conducive to romance.

As for me, I needed a wife. Legal, aboveboard. Even though I wanted a real marriage, we agreed it would be in name only. I'd avoided marriage all my adult life, dodging my parents' attempts to marry me off to some rich socialite bimbo. My father wanted the bank balance boost. I wanted freedom.

From the moment Synn began her protection contract for me eleven months ago, she was more than my bodyguard. She was my plus one at functions. She never let me down. She's one in a million.

I know she's going to hunt me down sooner rather than later. I've taken too long to contact her. It's been far too long since I've seen her gorgeous body and that smile.

After she left for her next assignment, death threats started arriving. At first, I thought it was Leo's mess. Now I'm not so sure.

With pride on the line, I wanted to prove I could protect myself. But I cringe at the thought of what Synn will do when she sees me. Maybe I should invest in a steel plate for my balls. I didn't even give her my new number.

The scent of the ocean fills my nostrils. Waves break against the pier. I refocus on why I'm here — hiding behind stacked crates, camcorder recording the three men in front of me for the past ten minutes.

Their voices carry in the still night air. "Everything is set. The assassination will take place tonight."

Oh shit. Assassination tonight.

The shortest man, slicked-back hair, husky smoker's voice: "You better. I've bankrolled this little outing too long. I want the Bianchi men gone."

Shit. I thought Leo was the target. Now I know better.

Over the last two weeks, I realized our guards were replaced with strangers. Our security is bogus. Tonight's gala — Leo's engagement party — is bait. Our plan was to uncover the mastermind. Now I have video evidence. Time to alert my family.

My wife's words about our lack of security echo in my head. As usual, my father refused to listen.

At times like this, I need her. Images of Synn in her tight black leather outfit, weapons strapped everywhere, like a sex goddess model. Her curves, her legs — strong, toned, flexible. I remember them wrapped around me.

Dammit. Not now. My dick grinds against my suit pants, seeking escape. Just thinking about her makes me hard. My dangerous girl has me pussy-whipped. I don't just miss her body. I miss her heart. Her soul.

Thanks to her, Leo and I have safe houses. She taught us to approach every event seriously, strategize, always have a backup plan.

The men's voices fade as they walk along the pier. At least I know what the Apolo Syndicate has planned. Time to warn Leo.

I squint, focus on the shorter figure. Seconds pass. He turns. What the... heck. I duck back. He climbs into a car. Not a man — a woman in a suit. That explains the voice.

Engines start. Cars leave. Who the hell is she? And why target my family?

I wait, then pull my cell. Notification.

LION:

The Phoenix has landed and carrying cargo.

What the fuck? The only person we ever spoke about in code like this was Essy — she is the Phoenix. What does he mean by cargo?

ME:

What cargo?

Three dots. They wiggle. Then:

LION:

WTF? Is that really your first question?
Not — how is the Phoenix?

Is he serious? I want to know the cargo.

ME:

FO. If the Phoenix is there, then they're
okay. What cargo?

Dots...appear. Wiggle. Then:

LION:

Looks like the last Phoenix visit — left
with a Kinder Surprise.

If I didn't know any better, I would swear my
brother is informing me my wife is pregnant. Pregnant?
Impossible. We used protection. She'll rip my balls off if
it's true.

I think back to her last cryptic message. Finally, it
makes sense. Oops. I squeeze my legs together and
groan. I'm in trouble.

Back to the mission. Time to warn Leo.

ME:

Time to order stationery. Send memo
to Phoenix.

LION:

Roger that. Already ordering.

Thank God. Synn won't mess around when she
realizes security is compromised.

Another message arrives.

LION:

Phoenix is hot.

WTF. If Leo touches my wife, I'll kill him. Just because the ceremony required the three of us... I wonder how much she remembers.

Stupid family curse.

My brother should kiss her feet. She saved our lives that weekend. Without the ceremony, we'd be dead.

I think of my father's twin, Uncle Zaiden, who died after Jaiden married my mother. Leo and I wouldn't risk it. Synn agreed to join us. She didn't know whether to believe us. But she went along, silent, while we chanted words during certain acts, surrounded by candles. I'm amazed the place didn't burn down.

Men in our family either live or die before their time. I'll cherish Synn forever for her sacrifice.

My fingers fly over the screen.

ME:

Get your head in the game and leave Phoenix alone.

Leo replies instantly. Double ding.

LION:

Touchy

LION:

Phoenix is asking for you.

Now that my wife is with my brother, it's time I catch up with them. Another ding vibrates in my hand.

My breath hitches, pride swelling in my chest. Of all the things my brother has ever texted me, this one I'll actually cherish.

My annoying brother has taken a photo of my beautiful wife.

I savor the image, drinking in her beauty. Oh, my gawd — she's pregnant. My eyes nearly bulge out of my head. How pregnant is she? I scan again, zeroing in on the protruding bulge, her hand mid-caress over her belly. Then I see it... my ring. My family ring. The one I gave her, told her never to take off. It's right there on her finger.

My lips twitch, a smile breaking wide. God, I love that woman. My heart and soul ache to hold her, to feel her wrapped in my arms. When I see her face-to-face, I won't hold back. She needs to know how much I want her, how completely in love with her I am. No more hiding our marriage from my parents. I know they're up to something, and this time I'll stop it.

I trace her picture one more time. How the hell did Leo snap this mid-surveillance without her noticing? He's right, though. She is hot. And she'll wring his neck if she finds out he took it. My girl is private.

Before I can talk myself out of it, I forward the photo to my secret personal account. Yeah, I know — paranoid much. But with my family, paranoia is survival.

Chapter Four

ESSY

Finally, two security personnel in their standard black suits appear from a side door. If I were in charge, I'd start by replacing these two clowns for their tardiness.

Actually, scratch that — I'd replace all of Leo's current security. What the hell has been happening since I left? Laini moves to my side, keeping pace with my steps.

Leo nods to his approaching detail as we head toward the gala exit. Caroline's annoyed tones fill the air within seconds, demanding to join us.

Leo shakes his head, keeps his back to her. Then I notice a cell phone in his hand. His fingers fly across the screen, and his face twists into that smug look I know too well. He slips the phone into his jacket pocket.

I know that face. He pulls it every time he's antagonizing his brother. So... is my annoying brother-in-law texting my husband?

Fine hairs rise along the back of my neck,

foreboding crawling higher. I glance around, and it clicks. Leo's in danger. We need to get out.

Warmth surrounds my back, dragging my focus to our exit. Leo needs to remember he's my brother-in-law, nothing more, as he places his arm behind me. People are staring, wondering who I am and why Leo is hovering like a helicopter parent.

"Leo, where are we going exactly?" I hiss, scanning left and right.

The urge to bolt spikes as tingles explode along my neck and back.

Whenever I get those sensations, I don't ignore them. I focus. "As I said, Sweets. Upstairs. What we need to discuss is confidential," Leo murmurs, urging me toward the elevators off the foyer.

I glance over my shoulder as we walk the brightly lit tiled path. Leo drifts away from his security, widening the gap. Brilliant. Let's just make ourselves easier targets.

Just as he presses the up arrow, I demand, "So, who is Caroline?"

"Ahhh. I wondered how long it would take you to ask." He smirks. "Are you jealous, Sweets?"

The urge to smack him upside the head is overwhelming. Thankfully, the elevator arrives with a ding, saving his face from my fist.

"Leo, stop being obnoxious and answer the bloody question." I usher Laini in ahead of me, then glance over my shoulder.

Two of Leo's guards stand with three strangers I

spotted earlier. If I didn't know better, I'd say those strangers are armed. Time to move.

"Leo…" I whisper. "Who are the three men down the hallway? One of them has a red hanky in his tux pocket."

With a nudge to my back, I step into the elevator. Leo glances toward the men, then says, "Keep moving, Sweets." He hits the close button and taps several floor buttons.

"What is going on, Leo?" I demand. I know that ploy — either get out two floors up or ride longer to confuse whoever's watching. He sends another message, pockets his phone.

"Look, Sweets, for all appearances, Caroline is my fiancée."

Who is he fooling? I bite back a snort. "Does Caroline know the engagement is not real?"

Leo shakes his head. Figures. What game is this family playing?

The elevator stops on the first floor. He dashes out. I hold the door, step forward, and catch him leaning into another elevator, tapping buttons, then rushing to the next open one, repeating the trick before the door closes.

He slips back into ours, and I hit close. Just as the doors nearly shut, another elevator dings. We're being followed.

Leo better know what he's doing.

He sighs as the doors close and the elevator moves. His puzzled glance flicks from Laini to me, then back to her. He's wondering who she is.

Time for introductions. "Leo, this is my sister Laini Raiker." His face shows surprise, then he nods. "Laini, this is Leo Bianchi."

Her eyes widen. She nods, turns to me. "Isn't he your old client? The super-rich dude?"

I shrug. "Kind of," I murmur, watching the numbers change above us. "His brother Declyn was the one who hired me."

Before Laini replies, the doors open. Leo darts out, catches another elevator, taps buttons, then races back before the doors close.

Our elevator stops on the second-last floor. He urges us out, presses more buttons, then exits himself. Laini stays quiet, glued to my side.

"This way," he says. "We'll enter the private elevator." He taps his watch, and a door further down the hallway swings open. "Quickly now."

Inside, he jabs the close button several times. At least he's watching his own back. Small miracles.

Okay... where are we heading?

I glance at him, murmur, "Is it safe to speak, or are we being watched?"

Leo watches the floor numbers climb. "Another minute, and it should be safe. Thanks for understanding," he whispers.

The elevator jolts, stops, doors sliding open. Leo steps out, scans the area, then reaches back for my hand.

"Come on, Sweets. We must keep moving." Geez. Who does he think he's with! I'm the bodyguard — the professional, not him.

I step out, noting coral-painted walls and dark carpet. Where has he dragged us now? I scan for threats, find none, and keep moving with Laini at my side.

"Sweets, we're nearly there," Leo murmurs. "How are you feeling?"

I raise a brow, stare straight ahead, trying to figure out our destination.

"Tired. Sore feet," I sigh. The urge to wiggle my toes and swirl my foot grows stronger. "You know, the usual when you're pregnant."

He shakes his head. "No, I don't. I'll take your word for it."

What in the world?

I was busy texting my brother one minute, and now I am waiting for him to answer the next.

What is going on?

He better be looking after my wife.

As I pass the slow cars along the busy freeway, concentrating on driving, I increase my speed. The need to see my wife with my own eyes grows with each mile I travel. I had better arrive at the safe house before my brother. The further I drive, the more my instincts inform me to change directions. I am sure the two vehicles behind me are the same ones I spotted ten miles back.

I maneuver around another vehicle and watch in my review mirror; sure enough, those two cars copy what I do and keep the exact distance between us. So I zip around three more vehicles to increase the space, only for the two cars to maneuver closer.

At the last second, I swerve and exit an off-ramp. I increase the throttle's pressure, my foot flat against the accelerator, listening to my V8 sports motor roar as the speed more than doubles as I dodge the slow cars.

As I scan my surroundings, I continue to look for the name of the road I need to take. Thank goodness I know exactly where I am. As soon as I see the sign, I turn down a side street, and just as quickly, I drive into the next road on my right and then every second side street to increase the distance from those two distinctive cars until I can change over to another vehicle.

My heart races as I approach the entrance to a storage facility. I pause long enough to enter the digital code Synn had me memorize before zooming through the half-open sliding gates along the smooth pavement and taking the chance and glance over my shoulder towards the front gates. When I see they have closed and no other vehicles are in sight, relief hits me. By the time I reached the second line of storage sheds, I'd turned off my headlights, and my car was less discoverable with any luck.

Out of sight from the road, I slowly approach the roller door with a big painted eighteen on it. With a quick swivel of my head, I glance around again for anyone or another vehicle. Then, with the coast clear and leaving the engine idling, I step out of the car, enter the code into the electronic keypad, listen to the lock disengage, and the gears crank. It is not long, and the automatic door moves and rolls up, opening to reveal a dimly lit area with a large object covered with a dark tarp.

Automatically, I run my hand up and over, flicking a set of switches inside the wall, lighting up the large enclosed area. Once my eyes adjust to the brightness, I notice extra boxes strategically stacked against one wall. The back wall comprises shelving containing different equipment, backpacks, various items, and weapons. To my right, a little office has been set up with two large office desks with various office equipment, including laptops and printers, filling a small portion of the wall.

My attention is then drawn to the tarp in front of me, a thick, dark covering shielding my wife's sports car. She fearlessly drove her beloved car, ensuring the safety of both Leo and me.

Gripping a fist full of smooth material, I tug, pull, and slide the tarp from the sleek black sports Audi R8, exposing my wife's pride and joy. I finish gathering the large tarp to one side and up onto a wall hook, keeping it clear of the car tires. Racing to the back of the storage room, I grab three backpacks and the car fob from a hook on the back shelf.

I release the Audi's rear hatch and place the backpacks in the car before closing the back. Next, I open the driver's door, slide in, set my foot on the brake, lift the key fob, and press the start button.

The dashboard lights up, and the engine turns over, coming to life with a roar. As I prepare to drive this beast of a car, I can already feel the engine's hum and the steering wheel's vibration in my hands.

Synn would be proud to hear her baby purr. She loved this car, with its bulletproof glass and panels. She would sit in the driver's seat, listening to the engine with a huge smile.

I slide the car into its reverse gear and carefully drive it out of the storage locker beside my idling car. Within two minutes, I have my car parked in the locker, and just as I go to flick the overhead lights off, I grab one of the full first-aid medical bags and a bagged laptop.

I was amazed when Synn explained how she could afford her sporty car, this storage space, and everything inside. Synn learned all about the stock market from an early age.

She started with five hundred dollars, and all these years later, including investment properties, she has a valuable nest egg worth hundreds of millions of dollars, probably a lot more. Per Synn's wishes, I have never mentioned to Leo or anyone else that my girl is exceptionally wealthy. So, why she continues to work has me stumped.

With a flick of my wrist, the lights turn off. I lift the two bags higher within my grasp as I hit the roller door close button, setting the alarms as I walk back to the Audi. I place the bags in the back before sliding into the driver's seat.

I fasten my seat belt around me and adjust the mirrors before driving toward the exit. As I hit the window button to access the exit keypad terminal, my cell phone pings to inform me that I have a new message.

I quickly glance down and discover a message from an unknown number.

UNKNOWN:

You will not escape. We will find you.

Chapter Six

ESSY

With Laini at my side, I'm amazed she's kept quiet this long. If I were in her shoes, I'd be firing off twenty million questions and refusing to take a single step until I had answers. But the look in her eye tells me she's listening carefully, soaking up every word between Leo and me. She knows we're in danger. It's just a matter of time before her avalanche of questions buries me.

Since I was a kid, I've always asked hundreds of questions. I had to know what was going on, what was happening. My mind worked a hundred miles an hour, strategizing what I thought I needed to do. It started back when I was stuck in foster care.

I lived from one foster home to the next. It never occurred to me that foster families didn't appreciate my constant questions. Some homes booted me after only a few days. Later, I realized my nosiness uncovered shady people who used and abused kids.

It was with my last foster family that I discovered

they were into child trafficking. During biweekly meetings with my caseworker, I mentioned overhearing conversations I didn't fully understand. I also told her what I glimpsed on Harvey's computer — my foster dad's desk. Let's just say the police showed up with a warrant. I was quickly transferred to the city orphanage.

A couple I'd never seen approached me in the orphanage gardens. Something about them felt different. When I shook their hands, I knew I could trust them.

Turns out, they were FBI agents looking for kids of specific ages to join a unique program. When they asked about my parents, I explained I didn't have any and was stuck in the system. Sadness crossed their faces before shifting to understanding.

With their connections, I was finally out of foster care and adopted, becoming Essynda Raiker. They introduced me to a man I thought was my new uncle but turned out to be their boss. Uncle Nigel.

Weeks turned into months, and I became engrossed in martial arts training and fighting techniques. Whenever I sat at a computer, hacking and reprogramming came naturally. Like a duck to water — or in my case, a duck with attitude.

Life became exciting. Learning about topics I never knew existed was fun. The deal was simple: keep my grades up in public school, and I could continue training at FBI headquarters. My parents were proud of my thirst for knowledge. I learned early on to keep my secret life... secret.

"So, Leo... I take it we're heading somewhere else," I casually ask, scanning the area.

Leo pauses, glances over his shoulder at my body, down to my shoes, then meets my eyes.

"Come on — this way. You'll like this." He presses part of the fancy wooden sculptured wall. A hidden button clicks, and the wall slides open, revealing a secret elevator. Sneaky. If I hadn't seen him tap it, I'd never have noticed.

"Come on. We better hurry." Ha. Leo might finally be learning about safety. What am I thinking... Dekk probably discovered this elevator first.

Laini and I step into the small space, moving aside for Leo.

"Leo, program your brother's number into my cell and any other number we'll need. Once we're out of this box, we'll toss your phone," I declare.

Leo raises a brow. "You must be slipping, Sweets. Usually, you'd have already organized that move."

"Look, smartass. If I'd had a heads-up, I would've said it back in the first elevator." If I didn't need this annoying man, I'd smack him. "A bit of info would be nice. Don't keep me in the dark again," I bite out.

I hand him my phone. He programs numbers quickly. Meanwhile, I slide his cell out of his pocket. Phew. My pickpocket skills are still sharp. With a flick of my wrist, I pop off the back, yank the sim and battery. Snap. The sim breaks in half. I close the phone, snapping the cover back.

The elevator stops. Doors open to a bright, empty foyer. Leo steps out first. I signal Laini to follow. As I step through, I drop the broken sim down the elevator shaft. Once I know where we're headed, I'll ditch the battery.

"Seriously, you had to destroy the sim already?" Is Leo serious right now?

I resist the urge to roll my eyes. Instead, I glance at Laini. She's opening and closing her hand, irritation etched across her face. Her fist tightens, knuckles white. She looks ready to knock Leo flat.

To save him from my sister's right hook, I change the topic. "When did you get suspicious of your security, Leo?"

He glances back at me, then at Laini, then forward again. "I thought Dekka was paranoid two weeks ago. Then, last week, I noticed completely different guards. Dekka reminded me of what you said about safety."

"So this is why we're bunny-hopping elevators. We're leaving the building." Not a question. A statement.

"Yes," he says.

"Leo, get moving. I need to get off my feet."

He pauses, eyes lingering on my belly before finally walking along the corridor's left side.

Chapter Seven

DEKK

Close to the city's outskirts, I know I have to change vehicles again. Synn explained the procedure when she was my bodyguard. 'You never know who is watching. Stay prepared. Only trust yourself when the enemy is close to home.'

I have valued her thoughts and wisdom. Leo and I had struck gold when Synn literally fell into our laps all those months ago. An old business acquaintance had mentioned a woman for hire in security with various skills.

She can be anything you require for private security. Somehow, she had agreed to take me on as a client. Synn became invaluable while traveling interstate. Don't get me started on the unwanted advances by desperate women willing to do anything to grace your bed and empty your wallet. Synn had taken pity on me and kept at my side, preventing a firestorm of malice women hitting on me or the business associates hostilities when it came to their company being taken over.

My annoying brother Leo thought it was his chance to be a dick and sleep with her. But in true Synn style, she set him in his place and acted professionally at all times. Well, until I got under her skin on her days off and the weekend we were married.

Leo and I might be identical, but for some unknown reason, Synn preferred me. The attraction between us has always been heavy and thick with sexual electricity. Just one touch from her, or when she would caress her bottom lip with her tongue, my dick would be ready for action.

The woman wove her spell over me and crept into my heart and soul.

I have kept one eye on the road and the other in the rearview mirror for the last ten minutes. As far as I can tell, no one is tailing me, and I continue to turn down several other side streets and cut across a freeway or two until I am five minutes from the safe house.

My safe house.

*B*eing the first to arrive, I entered my house, secured it by locking the door and activating the security alarm, just as Synn had instructed. The room is filled with silence, making me acutely aware of the absence of sound. My thoughts go straight to Synn and how much I have missed her. When will Leo arrive with my wife?

Synn's car was securely parked in my double garage, right next to my BMW M8. With bags at my feet, I slowly scan the room as I turn. Memories of my wife when we were both here last come rushing back. The anticipation of holding her in my arms again is overwhelming. There's a lot of information to share with her.

Even though I've been away for a while, I can still smell her favorite fragrance in the air. Given that Synn is in the state, there's a chance she came to the house, resulting in a possible message for me in the secret kitchen safe box.

I enter my kitchen and open the matching floor-to-ceiling cupboard doors. The cupboard has several shelves, and three of them swing out to reveal a hidden safe door. Thanks to Synn, there are three additional concealed wall safes, a panic room, and a secret exit within the house.

It does not take me long to enter the digital code, hear the metal lock release, and hear the hiss of the door opening. As soon as I open the door, I notice a sheet of paper on top of several items and lift it to read.

Hey Honey,
It's been a while, and we need to talk.
If you're reading this note without me, you must be here for reasons requiring a safe house to keep you safe.

If you have files on your cell, they must be copied ASAP onto the notebook computer.

Under the laptop, you will discover a pre-paid postal bag. Write your parents' postal address on it. Yes, you will post your cell phone, no ifs, and no buts—post it. Make sure to turn the cell off!

Also, inside the wall safe, you will notice another cell. I want you to plug it in and charge it.

My name and number are pre-programmed into it. Message me.

Keep safe.

Please don't take too long to contact me.

Love always.

Phoenix xx

My sexy woman might not be here physically, yet somehow, she still manages to look after me.

I reach back into the safe to remove the notebook computer, prepaid satchel bag, and cell phone with a power cord.

As per the notes instructions, I plug the power cable into a power outlet and connect it to the new cell phone to charge. Then, I open the notebook computer and press the power button, and once it's ready, I transfer the files.

I reach into my jacket pocket, pull out the memory

card from the small camcorder, and slide it into the laptop's card reader. Once again, I copy the files from today into a separate file. Finally, I open a new email, type in my secret email account, attach the files as zip folders, and hit send.

After gathering all the items, I switch off my cell phone, feeling a sense of detachment as I remove its back cover. With precision, I extract the battery, secure the cover back in place, and position both items inside the bag, sealing it. As I glance around, my eyes catch sight of a pen resting on the bench. Without hesitation, I grab it and inscribe my name and my parents' mailing address on the front.

Returning the notebook computer to the safe and closing the cupboard, next I check the new burner cell and notice the battery is almost fifty percent charged. I turn the cell on. A few seconds later, it lights up and does its thing before the home screen appears.

WELCOME DEKK.

Pops up, and my lips form into a smile. I tap the screen to contacts and notice five numbers programmed, one of which belongs to Phoenix. I do as the note says and tap a message to my wife.

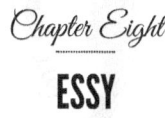
I stare in disbelief at the building in front of us as Leo drives into the attached garage.

This is not Dekk's safe house.

With another glance to my left and right. We're definitely in a run-of-the-mill suburb, identical houses with neatly trimmed lawns line the street, adding to my confusion as I try to figure out where the hell we are.

I turn my head and glare at Leo. He stops the car, kills the engine, and purposefully avoids eye contact. Without a word, he opens his door and steps out. The thud of the door closing leaves Laini and me boxed in.

My foot taps against the car's floor as my instincts kick in.

We need to move.

In disbelief, I watch Leo close the garage roller door manually. You have got to be kidding me. What is this, 1985? Next, he'll be rewinding VHS tapes.

I've scanned around us as we arrived. No additional

security. No cameras. No guards. Nothing. We're sitting ducks if anyone followed us.

That's it. I shove open my door and plant my feet on the concrete. "Leo, where are we?" I demand. "We are not safe here."

He strolls past the car toward the connecting house door. "What are you talking about, Sweets? No one followed us. Chill. Let's go inside and have a drink. Dekka should be here soon," he smugly rants over his shoulder.

Yeah, sure. Let me just chill while we sit here like ducks waiting for target practice.

My patience thins to a thread. I urge Laini to join me. Her annoyed look mirrors mine. She slams her door, the sound reverberating like a gunshot.

Laini steps beside me. "What does that idiot" — she jabs her thumb at Leo — "think he's doing? We are in danger here."

I nod. "Yep. Tell me about it. Come on, we better go inside."

We reluctantly follow him through the door into an average-looking single-story bungalow. Why do I feel we're going to regret this? The click-clack of my heels on polished hardwood echoes in my ears, followed by Laini's. The silence of the house swallows us whole. Where did Leo disappear to?

We step into a large, modern lounge room. I stop dead when I see Leo at a hidden wall safe. His back is to us. Of course. The aggravating man is selfish enough to ignore us while rummaging for God knows what.

Laini moves beside me, tapping her foot. My girl is not happy.

The echo of her tapping grows louder. She huffs, hands on hips, chin high. "Bathroom. Where is it?"

Classic Laini. She's got the bladder of a hummingbird and the patience of a rattlesnake.

Leo finally turns, glances at her, then at me. "Oh, right. I'd better show you both the bathroom." His gaze travels over us. "There's clothing for you to change into. Those gowns and shoes must be uncomfortable."

I nod, motioning for him to move. My bladder is screaming louder than he is.

Thankfully, it doesn't take me long. As I step back into the bedroom, Laini passes me, shutting the bathroom door with a click. I turn to the walk-in wardrobe and freeze.

Rows of clothes hang in perfect order. Shelves stacked with apparel, some still sealed in packaging. Why does Leo even have women's clothing in my size? Creepy much? Best not to ask. I grab something stretchy enough for my belly: thick black leggings, a black singlet, a men's dark blue dress shirt, a mid-thigh black leather jacket, and ankle boots in my size.

Laini moves behind me, unzips my dress, and lets it slide to the floor. The hairs on my neck rise. I glance back — Leo is watching through the door gap.

"Leo, you've seen me naked before. Pull your head out of your ass. Check the security. Lock the damn doors and windows."

Ignoring me, the annoying man barges in, door thudding open. His eyes lock on my belly.

I prop my foot on the bed, struggling with my heel buckle.

"Here. Allow me. I can do it," Leo mumbles, nudging my hands away.

His warm touch glides along my calf, down to my ankle. His head leans against my bulge. One twin presses against him.

He removes my shoe, sets it aside, lifts my other foot, and repeats the process. Then, before I can stop him, he presses both hands to my belly and kisses it.

"Hello, little one." The babe stops moving.

Excuse me? Brother-in-law privileges do not include belly-smooching. Try again, Romeo.

I slide my foot off the bed, stepping back from his wandering hands.

"Thanks for the help, Leo. Now leave and let Laini and me dress," I grumble. He needs to remember I'm married to his brother Declyn. "And, Leo, do you have weapons in this house?"

"We're safe here, Sweets. Don't worry," he says with that trademark smile, dimples flashing like he thinks they're bulletproof.

How many times do I have to remind him? I'm a trained professional. Safety comes first. He's not taking it seriously. I strip off my gun holster and dump it on the bed.

"Leo, if there are weapons here, collect them." I eye his tux. "And change. Lose the watch, too."

His smile fades when he realizes I'm not joking. "What is it, Sweets?"

He knows my game face. He's seen it before.

"Leo, we are not safe here. Someone could have followed us. Get changed. Grab cash. Put your wallet, watch, and cufflinks in the safe. We need to leave."

My mental checklist scrolls.

Safety. Protection. Weapons.

Leo just sits there, listening. The fool thinks we're safe. We're not. I grab his lapels, yank him to his feet. "Leo, move. Change. Grab weapons. We're leaving." I shove him toward the door.

Once he's out, I slam it shut. Laini stands there, hands on hips, eyes blazing. Uh-oh. My sister wants answers.

I walk up, signal her to turn so I can unzip her dress. She presents her back. "So when did Leo see you naked?" She shakes her head. "...Second thoughts, never mind."

I sigh.

"You're not going to like what I'm about to say."

Hairy monkey balls. This is not how I wanted her to find out. I pictured drinks at home, not this circus.

"Probably not," she says. "Just spill, Essy."

"Okay. But I warned you." I unzip her dress. "I'm married to Leo's twin brother. His name is Declyn."

"You're what...?" she screeches. I grab her shoulders to stop her spinning around. "Since when are you married — Ms. Too-Busy-For-Love," she mocks, pretending to shoot targets with her hands.

I wince. She's right. I swore I'd never marry. Too busy. Too focused. Until now.

Instead of a big fancy wedding, Dekk and I had a small, intimate ceremony.

I return to the bed, grab clothes, start dressing. "Laini, Declyn and I have a marriage of convenience."

"What...?" She straightens, eyes disappointed. "You married a guy you don't love?"

I flinch. She knows me too well.

"I do love Declyn. I've just never told him. He needed my help, and I gave it." I slide into the shirt, buttoning slowly. "He and Leo were dealing with family drama, and...I was there."

"What are you saying, Essy?" Her eyes flick to my belly. "He has a lot to answer for. He left you pregnant, for freak's sake. He hasn't been in your life all this time. So where the hell is he?" She yanks on her jeans, furious.

Yeah, well. I've asked myself that same question too many times.

I tug the leggings up, snug around my belly.

"Laini, no one knows we're married. Apart from the pastor, his wife, their daughter, her husband, and Leo. But he doesn't count." I slip into socks, squeeze into boots. "Look, can we discuss this at home?"

With a sigh, she nods. "This is not the last of this conversation, you know!" She pulls her hair free from her long-sleeved black top and reaches for the brown leather jacket.

"Yeah, yeah. I'll explain everything when it's safe." I change the subject. "Anyway. How was your trip to Australia?" Time to figure out what's made my sister so sad.

Laini shakes her head, sits on the bed, and hangs her head. "Heartbreaking," she whispers.

"Why? What happened, Laini? You were there longer than you planned."

She sighs, hiccups. Whatever happened has cut deep.

"I traveled to Melbourne. Thankfully, I arrived just in time to say goodbye to my good friend Cameron."

Oh, no. This does not sound good. I sit beside her and reach for her hand. "Why, what happened?"

She stares at the wall, squeezes my hand. "Over the last six months, whenever I could, I traveled back to Australia and stayed with Missy. While there, I visited Cameron during his treatment."

"Huh? Treatment? That guy's huge, fit, healthy as a horse!"

She shakes her head, swipes under her eye. "He discovered he had cancer."

"Ohhh. No."

She cuts me off. "Anyway, his treatment stopped working. He died last week. I left the day after the funeral to come home."

Nooo. Not Cameron. Poor Laini. Now I know why she delayed meeting me until today. She's only just arrived back in the country. "Ooh, Laini. Why didn't you say anything?" I wrap my arms around her. "I am so, so sorry." My embrace tightens. "At one stage, I was hoping you might get together."

She pulls back, shakes her head with a sad smile. "No. We discovered early on we were destined to be friends only."

I reach for my leg gun harness, strap it against my

thigh. "That's too bad. At least you know some men out there aren't jerks. Rare species, but they exist."

While I'm fastening the harness, Leo strolls back in, dressed down in snug black jeans, a pristine white shirt, and a trendy leather jacket. His feet? Shit-kicker boots. Typical Leo. He probably thinks he's bulletproof just because his shoes look like they could stomp a small country. Our eyes meet.

With a raised brow, I ask calmly, "Yes, Leo… What do you require?" He knows how good he looks. The annoying man knows how to push my buttons.

"Just to say, I'll bring you the weapons from my weapon safe." He disappears, then returns with arms full. He dumps a bundle of guns, harnesses, ammo, and knives on the bed. "Which ones do you require?"

Wow. What a collection. Either he's prepping for war or auditioning for an action movie.

I stand, select two G19 Gen5s and one knife. I wonder how he got all these weapons. Second thought — safer not to know. I motion for Laini to pick one, then face Leo. "Pick a gun. I taught you how to shoot. Don't let me down."

We check ammo cartridges, make sure they're loaded, then slide each weapon into holsters. I stash spare shells and clips in my jacket pockets.

After a few adjustments, a shoulder holster fits snug over my shirt, holding two G19 Gen5s. My G27 Gen5 straps to my thigh, and the eight-inch bowie knife hugs my calf, partly hidden by my boot.

I shrug into the long jacket. Fits like a glove, with

room for weapons. I signal the others to grab extra ammo.

I turn to Laini as she slides her feet into brown knee-length boots. She sits up, picks up a handgun, smiles, checks it over.

Proud. That's what I am.

Laini would've made a sensational agent.

She's come a long way since Chicago High School. Back then, she was Meredith Lewis, and I was undercover as a new student. We became fast friends when I saved her from cheerleader bullies.

My job was to collect evidence against her family for embezzlement and mob ties. The more I knew Meredith, the more I realized she and her mother, Dorothy, were innocent — trapped by her father Keith's mafia lifestyle.

The day Meredith's life changed forever, she was at my house. My parents came home early, interrupting our schoolwork. They broke the news: her parents were dead.

Dorothy and Keith were murdered, their house torched. Keith had double-crossed his partners, and they made him pay. The public was told the Lewis family perished in the fire.

Long story short, my parents placed Meredith in protective custody. We moved, changed her name to Laini Raiker. From that day, she became my sister. I taught her to fight, to protect herself, to use weapons.

My mind snaps back to the present. I strategize an escape plan. Trusting Leo was a mistake. How many times have I had to rescue him? With his tendency to overlook important details, he still believes he's always right. Spoiler alert: he's not.

Chapter Nine

ESSY

The sound of an incoming message breaks the silence. With a flick of my fingers, I light the screen up and see a text from my husband.

Thank goodness.

He's been to his safe house and using the burner phone I got him.

DEKK:

Hey, Phoenix. How's the cargo going?
It's time we talk.

Well... no shit, we need to talk, and I rub my belly.

ME:

Glad to see you using the cell. Did you follow all the instructions?

DEKK:

Yes. Where are you?

ME:

In Leo's den.

DEKK:

Ok.

ME:

Do you have my car?

DEKK:

Yes. Do you need it?

ME:

Yes.

Well. Well. So Dekk has been to the storage facility. I wonder what else he picked up while there.

DEKK:

I will see you soon. R U I D?

Are You In Danger? Wow! I wasn't expecting him to remember that one.

ME:

Are you serious? Leo has taken me somewhere I don't know. What do you think?

DEKK:

Leo is stupid.

I chuckle. My Dekk knows Leo is walking on thin ice with me.

ME:

> You're not wrong. A little assistance would be nice right about now. Having tingles.

I hope Dekk does not panic when he remembers what my tingles mean, especially when he knows to take them seriously.

DEKK:

> I'm coming. Amor Mio, Synn.

Chapter Ten

DEKK

*M*y stupid brother is at it again. He can make it hard to love him when he behaves the way he does.

No longer in my monkey suit, and I feel more myself now. Dressed in my go-to jeans, a shirt, my usual black leather jacket, and my favorite steel-capped black boots.

Now I know where my wife is. I place the last bags back in my wife's car, including *her go-to handguns and ammo*. I double-checked that all windows and doors were locked and the electronic security was fully activated before sliding back behind the wheel of Synn's car and starting the ignition again.

Five streets away from my safe house, I notice a 24-hour postal service, two men busy unloading one of the street post boxes. I pull up around the corner. It does not take me long to grab the satchel containing my cell phone and approach the two postal workers filling their van's back with bags, envelopes, satchels, and all-sized parcels.

I quietly whistle as I approach the two men so as not to surprise them. "Excuse me. Am I able to add another prepaid satchel to your collection?" I ask in a hurried voice, keeping eye contact with both men. "I hope I have not missed the chance to post my nephew's parcel. When I noticed your postal van and box... I've been stuck in meetings all day..." Once again, I leave my sentence hanging, hoping they will take the hint and take my satchel.

The postal man on my left eyes his partner and nods his head in a silent — *yes, we'll take it.*

Thank goodness! I can get rid of it.

The second guy grins and turns to me. "Sure, buddy. Just place it in the tub here. A few more minutes, and you would have missed us."

I quickly drop the satchel on top of the other mail, taking a step back. "Thank you, man. I appreciate you taking it. My wife would have skinned me alive if I had missed the mail." I smile and nod to both men, hoping my acting skills are up to scratch. Both postal men laugh at my fake predicament. "Thank you. Have a good evening," I say and walk off across the street, feeling their eyes watching.

After walking further up the road, I change direction and head back to the car. I'm not taking any chances with my safety. If either of the postal men sees the vehicle I'm driving... and if they somehow are questioned. The less knowledge they know, the safer we will be.

As I settle into the driver's seat, I carefully scan the

surroundings before securing my seat belt. With a push of the ignition button, I casually drive away.

As I drove, I kept one eye on the rearview mirror, ensuring I wasn't being followed. It was then that I calculated I was just twenty minutes away from Leo's safe house. I better send Synn a text. Thank goodness for Bluetooth and hands-free technology, which allowed me to speak my message and have it sent as a text.

ME:

20 out. How is everything?

It does not take long for Synn to reply, and the automated voices fill the car's speakers.

PHOENIX:

If you could make it 5, you'll make my day.

Oh, shit. What in the hell...? If Leo is not dead by the time I arrive, I might just kill him myself.

ME:

I'll be there ASAP.

Chapter Eleven

ESSY

*a*s we stand in the kitchen, the aroma of freshly brewed tea fills the air. Watching Laini, I can't help but wonder if she squeezed in a visit with her daughter Em before our appointment this morning.

Since her unplanned pregnancy at seventeen, my sister had kept her young daughter hidden from the world. It wasn't until a couple of years ago that I discovered I had a niece. The identity of Emma's father is still unknown, as Laini has chosen to keep silent about him. In her international public life, my sister is known to be single and without any children.

"Laini, did you see Emma last night?"

She glances towards the doorway before looking back at me with a nod. "Yes. After losing Cameron, I had to see and hold my daughter, you know."

I don't know how my sister is holding it together right now. I would be a mess.

"What are you going to do regarding your daughter? You can't keep her in hiding forever."

She sighs, washes her cup in the sink, and reaches for mine.

"Essy, you know my life is not straightforward." She pauses and shakes her head. "Anyway, next month, I'll be handing in my resignation. Thanks to your knowledge and skills in the stock market, you made us extremely wealthy women. We are financially secure and have ample funds to live comfortably for the rest of our lives."

Thanks to Laini's birth mother placing over two million dollars in an offshore bank account for her, Laini has not had to worry about money.

Laini turns, drying her hands on a dish towel. "Plus, my writing and books are excelling. My new book is coming out soon."

Uh-oh. A new book? The question is...have I seen the manuscript? "That is fantastic. Congrats on your new book release. Have I read it?"

Smile. Show her how happy you are for her.

I don't remember reading any of her new work this year.

Laini shakes her head. "Apart from when we discussed details about several characters. No. You haven't read the manuscript." I nod. Okay. Yet, I feel I've let my sister down. "There is something I would appreciate your help with, though." I smile and nod again. Okay. I'll do anything to make it up to her. "I would like to introduce Emma to Dad and Mom in a few months."

Wow. I nod in agreement and pass her my cup. Our parents are going to be surprised, especially our father.

I knew it!

It did not take long for Leo's so-called safe house to be discovered. Four armed people dressed in black army fatigues are outside the house. With the interior lights off, I stealthily stand beside the window. I peek from behind the curtain and notice two more men attempting to head to the house's backyard — hairy monkey balls.

"Psst. Leo," I quietly hiss. "Get your ass here."

Leo looks up from his coffee with a '*What do you want*' look.

With a handgun in my hand and the safety switched off, I point it toward the window. I flick my other hand, indicating for him to approach low.

Leo comes up and attempts to peek around me through the small gap in the curtains.

"What is your problem, Sweets?" he whispers near my ear.

I glance over my shoulder and stare him in the eye. "We have company. So far, I have spotted six-armed, and they're moving in." I take another look through the curtain, monitoring the men outside. "You better have an exit route because we can't go out the front, and the back is about to be covered. So what is the plan, Leo?" I feel him flinch at my words.

"Sweets, we should have been safe here," he pleads.

"I warned you, Leo. I said we are not safe here."

Then, after making sure I have accounted for the armed men outside, I urge Leo to move away from the window with me. "Time to leave, Leo."

I glanced at Laini and signaled her to pick up our cell phones. She slips hers into her jacket pocket as she approaches me with an outstretched hand. I take my cell and turn the volume down to vibrate. Dekk sent another text informing me he was on his way in the last message. I don't know if I should feel worried or relieved that he is not stuck in this house. If anything happened to him, I would never forgive myself.

"Leo, please tell me you have a secret exit because we must leave now. I have to warn your brother," I demand.

Leo's I know what I'm doing attitude crumbles before me with a shake of his head.

"Sweets, we need to head to the spare bedroom at the back of the house. There is a secret door leading to an underground tunnel." Before Leo can say another word, I encourage Laini to go low and head to the back of the house. I follow her along the dimly lit hallway, with Leo behind me. "The next door on the right," Leo urges quietly.

Laini partially opens the door enough so we can slip inside. Once we are all in the dark room, I close the door behind Leo. "Now, where?" I hiss. "Do not turn on the lights. We have to keep quiet." Finally, my eyes adjust enough, and I carefully watch Leo move to what I would presume is the walk-in robe or bathroom.

Laini and I stick close to Leo as he moves into the walk-in-robe and slides aside the hanging clothes. Leo pushes against the shelving unit, and I hear a click. I watch Leo pull the shelving unit enough to form a doorway opening big enough for us to slip through.

"Leo, don't forget to slide the clothing back and close the doors."

Leo nods and encourages Laini and me to slip into a small chamber within the wall. The sound of the clothing moving along the rail, then the snick of the shelving, lets me know Leo is right behind me.

No windows to allow light in, and surrounded by the darkness, I tap my cell screen, illuminating our little area. I whisper, "Can you inform Dekk where we're headed." I pass Leo the cell. "He's on his way." While I wait for Leo, I scan the area, but there is no sign of a door, leaving me puzzled and uncertain. Frustrated, I demand, "Where is the exit, Leo?"

I turn in time to see Leo type something and hit send before he passes me the cell back. I glance at the screen when it lights up with an incoming text. Okay, let's see what the boys have been saying.

ME:

> Taking Phoenix via the secret exit.
> We're surrounded. Meet us at CS.

DEKK:

> You better keep Phoenix safe.

What and where is CS? I glance up to see Leo passing Laini several glow sticks. "Here. Activate them," he whispers.

She shakes and bends them, activating them. Leo

grabs several more from a little shelf to his right and shoves them into his pocket. Just as I am about to question him on his text, the sound of a door being forced open somewhere inside the house sets us all on alert. At least we know they have breached the house.

I hear Leo murmur, "Oh, fuck." He pushes past me and lifts the rug on the floor, moving it to the side, revealing a trap door. Leo reaches down and dislodges a small pull-ring handle. Within seconds, he opens the trapdoor and encourages Laini and me to get inside the hole.

Chapter Twelve

ESSY

*L*aini pulled out her cell phone and tapped on the torch app, instantly illuminating the dark hole. As the light spilled out, a ladder became visible on one side. After dropping several glowing sticks down the hole, she shoots a quick glance in my direction. Annoyed, she shakes her head and lets out a frustrated huff before carefully positioning herself on the ladder to begin her descent.

"Leo, grab the rug to cover the trapdoor as you close it," I whisper.

Nodding in agreement at what I said, he tells me, "Get a move on, Sweets," with a hint of urgency in his voice.

With caution, I maneuver onto the ladder. Thankful to Laini for keeping the ladder illuminated and placing her hand at my ankle, making sure each foot landed on the next rung of the ladder, making it safer for me to descend.

Above our heads, we can hear the sound of heavy-soled shoes running through the house. Leo steps down onto the ladder before I reach the bottom and carefully closes the trapdoor, canceling any noise from above.

The colored glow sticks on the ground emit a soft light, casting a partial illumination of our surroundings. My sister picks them up, passing me one. Leo pulls a couple more from his pocket and activates them, creating more light.

Leo turns and begins walking, and whispers over his shoulder, "Come on. This way."

Laini and I look at one another, and we shake our heads. Great. What choice do we have?

We hesitantly follow Leo down a narrow dirt tunnel with many bends and turns. We duck our heads in some parts, avoiding plant roots and low rough dirt ceilings. After what felt like an hour of unsteady walking, even though it was only a matter of minutes, my legs noticed a slight incline.

We better be near the end of this dark, horrid tunnel.

The stillness in the air was the first thing my brain noticed, as if the world had gone completely silent. The only thing racing through my mind was the fact that the armed men had not uncovered the safe room or tunnel. With each step we take, the lack of any noise from behind only adds to the mounting sense of danger and urgency. We need to get out of here as soon as possible.

Leo stops in front of a rough-looking door that blends into the rock and pushes against it. He grunts and uses his shoulder to slam against the door. It is not long, and I hear him swearing under his breath about something to do with a stupid door.

The silence is broken by a massive explosion somewhere behind us. We all duck low to the ground. Within seconds, the ground shakes and trembles.

"Oh fuck," Leo roars. He is soon on his feet, slamming against the stuck door harder than before.

"Get us out of here, Leo," I yell simultaneously, cradling one arm protectively around my belly and the other against the rough stone wall to keep me from falling.

"Hurry the fuck up, Leo. The tunnel is caving in," Laini screams as dirt, rock, and heavy, thick dust fill the tunnel behind us.

With a loud grunt, Leo opens the stuck door. Laini and I move forward and squeeze through the gap. As soon as we are clear, Leo presses his body through the narrow opening, turns around, and pushes back against the door, closing it shut to the falling debris of rock and dust.

We cough our lungs up for several minutes to clear the inhaled dirt. I wipe my hands over my body to dislodge dust and debris from my clothing and glance around us, taking in the scenery. Somehow we have arrived under cover of shadows. The brick building appears old and derelict from what little I can see. Broken windows are spaced and positioned high along the walls, allowing little light. Scattered about the space are broken furniture and crates. As I step forward, my foot brushes against what appears to be some form of bulky fabric. Closer inspections reveal it to be a sleeping bag. I glance around the area, only to notice several other sleeping bags and piles of blankets. It looks like we have come across a Squatter's refuge.

We begin to head for an exit, walking through the abandoned factory. We pause when we hear the sound of glass breaking, followed by far too many rushing footsteps crunching on more breaking glass — hairy monkey balls. We've run out of time, and Dekk is not here.

Something makes me glance toward Leo. The only way for those men to find us this easily is if Leo has a tracker on him. It's the only thing I can think of. Chances are he failed to remove everything, as I requested.

I signal to Laini and Leo. The sound of footsteps getting closer to our position is not good, and I motion them to keep low. Grab their weapons, and continue for the only exit in the opposite direction of whoever is after us.

With my Gen5 Glock firmly gripped in my right hand, I proceed as quietly as possible with my back against the wall, constantly scanning. With no protection, we were sitting ducks.

Laini moves in close, and we both look at the exposed ceiling with plenty of positions for a shooter to hide. A shadow moves enough for me to realize someone is up there. We both turn towards one another, and I hand signal her to monitor the shadow. With a nod of her head and her gun poised, she keeps her chin tilted up, watching the ceiling above us.

I trust Laini with my life. She is more than some

airhead chick who works for a glossy women's magazine. Laini is well-trained in self-defense and weapons. She could out-shoot, out-strategize, and take down my old partner — and he was ranked number two behind me before I started my private security business. I taught her most of what she knows.

My skills were invaluable while serving in a small, elite unit in the government military. The eighteen-month recruitment when required for secret missions. Our last deployment had extended to a two-week mission. Thankfully, all I'll say is we were successful, and we made it home alive.

During my covert deployment, I stumbled upon a shocking revelation — if anything were to happen to me, my parents would be fed a fabricated story. The mission would have been shrouded in secrecy, its true nature forever hidden. Making the decision to change my life and career, I tendered my resignation shortly after we arrived back on US soil, effectively concluding my full-time tenure with the FBI.

By changing my employment options to part-time with the FBI, I decided to use all my skills and experience and turn them into protective services as a bodyguard.

I remind myself to keep my heart rate steady and slow my breathing. I listen as hard as I can for any approaching footsteps. Right here goes. As fast as I can, I glimpse through the doorway. Only finding a small, darkened, shadowed foyer and a narrow corridor. Monitoring the area for threats, I reach for Laini and tug on her jacket. She taps my leg to let me know she has my back. I slip into the small foyer, glancing all about.

With the next area clear, I reach back through the doorway for Laini. Within seconds, Laini and Leo are right behind me in the foyer. As fast as we can, we move along the corridor until I can spot what I hope is the exit.

I stop, turn my head, and whisper beside Laini's ear, "Swap with Leo. I trust you more than him with your gun skills." I point up. "Watch that shadow in the rafters."

She nods. Then she whispers back, "Where are we headed?"

I feel one baby move and kick. The little bugger does not like me in this squat position. Well, guess what, kid... we have no choice! I rub my belly, hoping to calm the babe.

"Closest exit and somewhere outside. Fingers crossed, Dekk is waiting for us in my car." My husband better be out there. I reach back into my pocket, grab the cell, and quickly tap a text informing him we're heading towards an exit and we're surrounded.

"For our sakes, so do I," she whispers. "Keep safe, Essy."

I nod to Laini's words when I feel the vibration in my hand. Glancing down at the screen and see the incoming message.

DEKK:

Keep safe. 5 mins out.

ME:

XXX

Anxious to leave this place, I exhale deeply before tucking my cell phone away and grabbing my second gun. I hope we make it out alive, with my heart pounding and adrenaline coursing through my veins. If Leo somehow escapes being shot, I might just be the one to pull the trigger myself after the trouble he has caused us.

I give my sister a brief smile. "You, too, Laini. Love ya." She nods and smiles.

The sound of approaching footsteps crunching down on the broken glass brings my head up and around. Then, moving shadows appear — hairy monkey balls. We're in trouble.

Her smiling face quickly transforms into one filled with determination. "Laini, swap with Leo now. We have to move. Guns up."

As Laini moves, I sense the weight of a more substantial body taking her place next to me.

"What's going on? Why are we waiting?" Leo demands beside my ear.

"Why?" I turn my head and meet Leo's eyes. Is he serious right now? "We are surrounded, so get your gun ready. We're about to have a shootout for our lives," I hiss. I can see when reality sinks into his head. His eyes widen, and he swallows hard. He glances over his shoulder. probably looking for the bad guys. "Leo, watch above. They're in the rafters of this building. And shoot to kill." I watch him nod as he reaches for his gun, then lifts it in front of him. "And Leo... Dekk will be here soon." He shakes his head again and points his gun at something I cannot see.

Oh, boy. I just hope the idiot does not shoot Laini or me.

I hear the following sounds of guns being cocked, with several more incoming steps crunching on broken glass.

Dammit. Our time is up.

With the familiar weight in each hand, I ready myself.

When I notice movement, I raise my gun.

"Ready. Go," I whisper.

I push off the wall and begin squeezing the trigger. The echo of my firing gun surrounds us. I duck automatically at the shower of fast-flying bullets as bits of plaster and brick fly around us. Something big had hit the ground close by me. Fingers crossed, that is one less assassin we have to deal with.

I wait for the bullets to pause, and I sneak a peek around the corner. Meters away on the dirty floor is a body just lying there. I don't have time to think about who it might be as another shadow appears just up from me. I lift my gun and continue firing; another figure falls to the ground. I duck lower when a bullet misses where my head previously was. Hairy monkey balls, that was close. I scan behind me as I grab two new magazines full of shells and swap them in both handguns.

I am relieved that Leo and Laini are still firing their

guns into the shadows. At least I know they are alive, and Laini has my back protected.

I inch forward and scan the hallway. I notice movement again through an old broken interior window in the wall, aim and shoot, not just once but twice. The shooter falls and hits the ground bringing my tally up to three shot men, or is that four? Hard to tell, as I've also lost count of Laini and Leo's tally.

I shuffle back and reach for Leo. "Stop shooting for a second," I whisper. Leo and Laini cease firing, and silence fills the area. I strain my ears in the silence. It's quiet — too quiet.

My mind races with different scenarios. Either we have shot everyone, or the armed shadowed men are biding their time. I bet they are waiting to see if we have run out of ammo. Of course, they would kill us as soon as we moved out into the open.

Somehow, running out of ammo is not an option, nor is moving out into the open. I inch closer to the broken interior window, stretching my neck to give me a little more height.

I duck when a shadow moves in my line of sight. Then, with my gun ready, I prepare for the shooting to begin.

I begin a silent countdown in my head... Five, four, "Sweets, what's taking so long?" Leo demands beside me. He just about gave me a heart attack.

What the hell is going through his mind, standing there like an absolute moron? As soon as I hear the sound, I instantly move, my body reacting instinctively. As bullets spray around us, a sharp sting radiates from my shoulder, but I ignore the pain as I grab his jacket, forcefully pulling him down.

Stupid. Stupid man. When will he ever learn? If I hadn't grabbed him and pulled him to the ground, the bullet would have found its mark. Plaster and bits of brickwork rain down, landing on my head and shoulders. With my adrenaline surging through my veins, I keep firing. A relentless barrage of bullets fills the air, all originating from the same direction. My tally increases to six as I hear two more bodies hitting the ground.

Laini curses as she fires several shots again.

Leo is going to be lucky if we do not shoot him first. Why did he speak so loud and stand? The stupid fool is trying to get himself shot. I aim towards my next target, squeezing the trigger, hitting another figure, and sending him to the ground. My finger is already pressing against the trigger, sending another bullet or two at another moving shadowed figure, hearing an oomph and grunt.

I move to better my view, barely dodging a bullet near my head as I squeeze my trigger, shooting another gunman. Shit. If I had not moved, I would have been shot myself.

I pause long enough, swapping the spent magazines for fresh ones. Watching the rafters every few seconds, a moving shadow of a man appears with a shape of a gun aiming at us. I don't waste any time. I aim and squeeze the trigger.

The sound of a grunt is heard before he tumbles and hits the ground with a heavy thud. Next, I aim to my right. I spot another figure moving at the end of the hallway.

I awkwardly squeeze off another shot with my left hand. Uh-oh... That is strange. My left hand is not functioning as it should.

In my haze, it soon becomes apparent. My body is not responding fast enough to move. I might have hit the first figure, sending him down, but the person standing behind him fires a round of bullets before I can move. Dammit. My body jolts as hot pain spears through my upper chest, sending me backward with an oomph. I squeeze the trigger awkwardly as my knees buckle.

As the shooter crashes to the floor, I find myself sliding down the wall, my gun slipping from my grasp as I instinctively clutch my shoulder. Glancing at my hand, it takes a few seconds for my brain to process the sight — bloody hell.

You have to be freaking kidding me... Noooo.

My breath catches, and my pulse increases — warmth and stickiness coat my hand — what little light is enough to reflect off the wet, dark liquid.

Blood.

My blood. Why is there so much blood?

In seconds, the sound of another body hits the ground, followed by the silence of no shooting. I glance up as the air grows quiet.

My hand feels numb as my field vision darkens around me. Oh, this is not good.

Thanks to Leo, I'm dying.

"Help," I mumble.

My babies fill my mind. *I'm so sorry you didn't get to meet your daddy.*

Then the image of my husband fills my mind. *Dekk, I love you.*

"Essy." Laini's voice reaches my ears. "Ah, shit. No, no. Essy." I feel Laini at my side. "Essy. Essy, can you hear me?" she demands. The weight in my hand disappears, and the last thing I hear is, "Leo, grab Essy's cell phone and call your brother now."

Chapter Thirteen

DEKK

*T*he sound of the tyres screeching along the pavement fills the air as I bring Synn's car to a grinding halt next to the old derelict brick building. Opening the car door, I am immediately met with the sound of gunfire coming from the building.

No. I'm too late.

With one hand, I carefully close the car door, the sound barely audible. In my other hand, I grasp one of Synn's handguns, poised for any potential threat. I glance over my shoulders, scanning the surroundings for any signs of danger. With each passing second, the temptation to call out to Synn intensifies. My brain pauses enough for me to realize that if I did, I might risk Synn getting shot. I might be annoying, but I am not reckless, and move as quietly as possible toward the nearest door.

I take a few seconds to acknowledge that the sound of gunfire has stopped. My heart speeds up, and my anxiety grows. Synn better be okay, or my brother is a dead man.

The vibration of the cell phone in my pocket begins. I pull it out and notice it is an incoming call from Synn.

"Baby, where are you?" I demand as I pull on the door handle.

Instead of hearing my wife's sexy voice, similar deep tones of my brother fill the line. "Dekk, where are you? Essy's shot." I freeze in motion as the door swings towards me.

"She's what?" I scream down the phone. "Where in the fuck are you guys?"

"Dekk, shut the fuck up. We are in the building surrounded by dead guys. Essy needs medical. Now."

I stop walking and pause long enough. "I'm here. So don't shoot me."

"Hurry the fuck up, Bro. She's unconscious," Leo shouts.

I move the phone away from my ear. Leo's voice echoes through the building as I take off as fast as possible. At least I know I am in the right building.

I notice a dim light ahead and, with caution, head that way. The smell of blood hits me before I come across bodies on the ground.

Oh, shit. Who in the hell are these guys?

The quiet tones of a female cursing at my brother inform me I am close in this maze of broken walls and concrete. I turn a corner and notice the illumination of a cell light with two people hovering over a person slumped against the wall further up a long hallway.

"Synn?" I say out loud. The two people look up. I

notice one is my brother Leo, and the other is a woman I do not know. Before I can take another step, the woman stands with her gun pointing straight at me.

I pause in mid-step and glance back at my brother. "Leo, are you going to introduce me to your friend?" I calmly ask, not knowing if the woman with the gun is a friend or foe.

Leo glances up at the armed woman. "Laini, this is my brother, Dekk." He then turns back to Synn before saying, "Dekk, this is Laini, Essy's sister."

"Sister...Laini?" My mind spins. I vaguely remember Synn mentioning she has a sister. Not blood. Adopted. I meet Laini's concerned eyes. "Laini, can you explain what has happened?" Hoping she is more intelligent than Leo. Okay, anyone is more competent than my brother.

She lowers the gun with a nod and drops to her knees beside Synn. "We were followed and then ambushed here. Essy had been protecting us, and dickhead here stood up at the wrong time. Essy pulled him down just in time to avoid being shot. But, as you can see, Essy was shot instead."

She pushes Leo's hands out of the way and lifts Synn's clothing. The sound of material ripping snags my attention. Frozen, I watch Laini applying the ripped fabric against Synn's wound. At least someone is thinking rationally.

Anger soon fills me. Knowing my wife has been shot because of Leo being reckless. Laini is right — he is a *dickhead*. If he were not my twin, I would shoot the idiot.

My feet finally move, and I rush over to my unconscious wife. I gently touch her face. "Hey baby, stay with me." My eyes roam over her body, and I notice her not-so-flat belly. Holy shit. Reality hits me in the face. My wife is pregnant. My hand shakes as it hovers over the protruding bulge. *Over my child!*

I shake my head and focus on what needs to be done. What would Synn do in this situation? I glance back to Leo. "Bro, use Essy's phone and snap some pictures of the dead guys. Knowing Essy, she'll want to discover who these people are." The faint sounds of sirens can be heard in the distance. Shit, someone must have called the cops. We need to leave. It's not the time to trust any strangers right now. I turn to my sister-in-law. "Laini, can you help me with Essy? I'll pick her up. Can you cover us in case there are any more shooters about?"

She nods and stands with her gun at the ready. By the looks of her, she knows how to handle a firearm.

The faint sound of beeping increases with each breath I take. The horrid odor of disinfectant hits my nostrils, reminding me of sickness. I flinch at the pain radiating from my upper chest and shoulder.

What in the hell... where am I? I must have moaned or moved, for someone had clenched my hand. Their touch...is familiar.

"Dekk," I murmur.

"Babe, don't move. You're in the hospital. You have been shot," my husband announces. Shot... how? Why? When? Then the realization — my babies.

I try to reach down to my belly when a pinch pulls at my hand. "Ow." Dammit, that hurt. What is wrong with my hand?

"Essy, the twins are okay." He squeezes my other hand again. "They are safe and sound in your belly, my beautiful wife."

Despite the heaviness in my eyelids, I muster all my strength to force them apart. Finally, after several attempts, they lift slightly. Annoying, harsh, blinding light floods my eyes, forcing my tired, gritty eyelids to snap shut once more. All I know is my dry eyes require eye drops.

I take a few extra seconds to comprehend what Dekk said. Did he just announce — my beautiful wife?

So what happened to keep our marriage quiet?

I hear a chair scrape along the floor, and Declyn releases my hand. Why is he moving? I have questions. Lots of questions.

"Dekk, why was I shot?" I croak. My throat is as dry as my eyes. How long have I been in a hospital?

I search my brain for any clue. What was I doing to be shot?

Not a single image or memory of why I'm here comes to mind.

Nothing.

"Here, Essy. Take a sip of water. You must be dry."

I nod and open my mouth slightly, allowing what feels like a straw against my bottom lip. I close my mouth and suck, taking a small sip. Once I swallow, I take a bigger mouthful, release the straw, and swish the water around my mouth before swallowing. Ah. That's better.

With a determined effort, I try again and cautiously open my eyes, taking in the world around me before I shield my gaze from the blinding brightness and fixate on the silhouette beside me.

After a few more blinks, the image focuses, and my sexy husband fills my vision with a huge smile.

"Hey, gorgeous. It's great to see you again," Dekk says before looking up.

"Thanks for the water, Dekk." Wow. My throat was dry, and turn my head to see what caught his attention.

My pulse increases when I see Leo.

Freakin' Leo.

Now I remember.

I attempt to sit up, only for Dekk to stop me. "Essy, you need to stay still."

You have to be bloody kidding me. Anger fills me as I glance back at my husband. "Declyn, this is my only warning — get your brother out of here," I demand. I glance to my other side. "Where's my gun? I'll shoot him." The sound of beeping increases somewhere behind me.

I wonder where my gun is and glance to my left and right again — no weapon.

I meet Leo's gaze and watch his face transform from smiling to sadness. "Come on, Sweets. I didn't mean to get you shot."

Seriously... that is his reason and lack of apology!

Counting to five in my head does nothing to calm me. "Leo, if you value your life, get the fuck away from me. Remember, I don't need a gun to end your life."

"Sweets, you don't mean that?"

"Leo, get the fuck away from me. I was shot because you kept me in the dark. You refused to inform me what was happening or where we were going. Plus, you stupidly stood up in the middle of a hostile situation. How dumb are you?"

I turn my head and notice my medical monitor numbers change and flash. Then, the blood pressure cuff on my arm activates, and a little alarm sounds not long after. Sure enough, I can see why. My blood pressure is increasing.

A nurse comes rushing in and checks over the monitors. "Right, everyone out. You are stressing the patient. I will not ask again."

I reach for the nurse. "I want my husband to stay, but I want his brother out. Do you understand me?" If I have to look at Leo again, I might just get out of this bed and wring his useless neck.

Dekk's voice fills the silence. "Leo, listen to my wife. Remember, she is my wife. You were meant to keep her safe, and look at what happened."

Wow. Dekk thought he could trust his brother with my safety. Fool him! Leo is one of the most self-centered men I have ever met. All he ever thinks about is himself.

"Come on, bro. I got her out of the gala."

"Leo, get the fuck out of here. Aren't you meant to be with your fiancée?" Leo flinches and casts his head down. "Mom and Dad will wonder where you disappeared."

I feel the warmth of Dekk's hand surrounding mine. I can tell by his shaky touch that he is keeping himself back from his brother.

Leo pauses at the doorway and looks over his shoulder. "Dekk, you know it was a sham of an engagement party. It was to draw out the people who are after me."

Dekk scoffs and curses under his breath, then replies, "Leo, you fool, those people are after our family. You stuffed up once again. Not me. I have been busy working undercover since my wife's been on assignment. What did you do... cause more trouble? And back to your fiancée—"

With a jeer, Leo haughtily murmurs, "Mom and Dad are going to find out about Essy."

"So what, Leo? It is time our parents met their daughter-in-law. Don't forget. She is carrying their grandchildren. They liked her before she became my wife. Never forget that."

Leo's shoulders sag, and a sigh leaves his mouth. He knows Dekk has him over a barrel. "But they had plans for you to marry someone else, Declyn," he whines. "They will not be happy discovering you married a woman, not of their choosing."

What the...? What is Leo going on about?

"Leo, get out of this room. If anything else happens to my wife or children..." Dekk didn't finish his words. There was no need.

The nurse has had enough. She urges Leo out of my hospital room with the door closing behind them.

Several seconds later, the door swings open again, causing me to glance at it. There in the doorway, I notice an older couple stepping through. Then it hits me. My parents-in-law have arrived.

Hairy monkey balls. How much of the conversation

did they hear? By the look on their faces, they had heard enough.

I glance back to Dekk, meeting his eyes with the look, *'we are in trouble now'*. He winks at me, then smiles before looking back towards his parents.

"Mom, Dad, what a wonderful surprise. What are you doing here?"

Chapter Fifteen

DEKK

The last thing I need to contend with is my parents.

All I want to do is wrap myself around my wife. Hold her and feel my children move about within her body. I've been stubborn long enough regarding my love for Synn. First, seeing her unconscious scared the crap out of me. Then, seeing our children on the monitor — alive and moving, relief filled me. How could I not love them all? I could have lost them.

While waiting for Synn to wake, I decided it might be wise to wait before mentioning to my wife that I love her. The last thing I want is to scare her and end things before we have the chance to be a family. We need time alone with one another. We need to talk.

At least her sister left to grab drinks for us. Plus, Laini had to get away from Leo. I don't blame her. I am incredibly close to punching him in the face myself. Even though I know they are adopted, the resemblance between her and my wife is uncanny.

When the doctors performed the ultrasound to check the babies' vitals earlier to ensure they were unharmed and healthy, I could not believe what I saw. I became speechless when looking at my children on the monitor. The doctor had sat there explaining what I was witnessing as he waved the transducer over my unconscious wife's belly. Finally, the doctor quietly murmured, we have monozygotic twin boys.

Boys!

I glance at my annoying parents with another deep breath, smile at Synn, and wink. I do not need her becoming any more upset than she already is, compliments of my selfish brother.

My father scowls and glances between Synn, and Leo, who is now just behind them, to me, then back to Synn.

"Essynda, a pleasure to see you again. I didn't know you were back?" my father stresses with a strange look.

As usual, my beautiful, skillful wife smiles at my parents. "Mr. and Mrs. Bianchi, I didn't know you were in town. Thank you for dropping by."

My mother pulls a face, and the gleam in her eye shows she will not drop the subject. "Essynda, dear," she purrs as her eyes rove over Synn's body and stop on her baby bump. "My, you have been busy. I didn't know you were married."

Synn casually releases my hand and rubs the side of her belly. It was then that I realized she had inadvertently displayed my ring. Mother's eyes widen as she looks from Synn's hand to mine, then back to Synn again, before setting her sights on me.

Oh, shit.

"Declyn, is there something you think your father and I should know?" Mother casually asks, even though I can see her left eye twitch. Yep. My mother is angry.

I reach for Synn's hand and squeeze it.

"Mom, Dad. Essy and I are proud to announce you will be grandparents. Isn't that fantastic?" I lean forward and press my lips to my wife's before facing my parents again. "You have wanted to become grandparents for a while now, and Essy and I have made that a reality."

Synn squeezes my hand hard. If I glanced down, her eyes would be like death rays, wanting to kill me. So I gently squeeze her warm hand back and stroke my thumb under her wrist.

My parents both splutter and trip over their tongues. I would laugh at their reactions if the subject were not so serious.

My mother finds her voice first. "Declyn, are you saying you have married Essynda and expect a baby together?" She points at Synn and lifts her chin. "Why is she in the hospital with a bullet wound? The woman should be at home safe and protected."

I cringe at her words. If I'd known of the pregnancy, I would have had my wife well-guarded in my home. She would not be out there on the street, working or whatever she had been doing all this time.

My father's face changes from bright to dull red. The vein at the side of his head has finally reduced in size as he attempts to get himself under control first. As his gaze flickers repeatedly between Synn and me. Ha. Now, that didn't last long.

His nostrils flare. "Declyn, when did you marry Essynda? Because the announcement for your up-and-coming engagement to Lucille will have to be placed on hold until we can sort out some form of annulment."

What the hell? I'm a grown adult. They will not tell me whom I should marry. No way would I annul our marriage. I love her, and I owe Synn my life.

I shake my head. "Sorry, Dad. I am not annulling my marriage to Essynda. She is my wife. We have been married for over six months. As you can see, we have had sex, which means the marriage has been consummated. She is very much pregnant with your grandchildren."

My father splutters once again, turning dark red. From the look of his nostrils, they are the widest I have ever seen them... don't even get me started on how his eyes are just about bulging out of his skull. "Declyn, the contracts were signed last week."

What the hell? Last week, I did not sign any marriage contracts.

I glance down at Synn. Her eyes are full of hurt and disappointment. She then gives me a dirty look.

What in the world is going on? I shake my head in disbelief. I have not agreed to or signed any contract. "No, Dad. I did not agree to or sign any marriage contracts last week. Why would I when I am already married?"

"Don't talk down to me, boy. You signed the contracts."

I'm afraid I have to disagree and glance at Leo, only to find he's left the room. Bloody Leo — It had to be him! "No, Dad. I did not. I was interstate last week on business, finalizing things in Nevada. Leo was the son you dealt with, not me. So take the contracts up with him. Plus, Leo knows I am already married. He was there the day I married Essynda."

How dare Leo sign marriage contracts pretending to be me when I am already married to Synn? What game is he playing now? Just wait until I get my hands on my twin. He is a dead man walking right now.

"Essynda, dear. Why are you in the hospital?" Mother asks. Too calmly — what is the woman up to?

I glance down at my wife, her eyebrow raises on her forehead as her eyes meet mine. Then she turns and smiles at my mother.

"Mrs. Bianchi, I was trying to catch up with Declyn when Leo escorted me from the gala. Long story short. We were followed and ambushed. I was shot, protecting Leo. If he had not stood up when he had, I would not have been shot. But, as usual, your younger son does not think. He continues not to listen. Because of that, I could have lost either baby or my life."

"I thought that was your job?" Say what? How dare my mother say that! Synn is pregnant. Synn's only job is to protect our twins and herself.

With a shake of her head, Synn replies, "Not when I'm officially on maternity leave." Synn glances at me, then back at my mother with a scowl. "Leo kept me out of the loop. He failed to inform me of what was going on. It was a miracle Leo wasn't killed." She glances at me again, then back at my parents. "If it were not for me, Leo would have died the night of the gala. Never forget that."

"What about his security?" my father smugly says.

Synn scoffs. "Really? Do you think Leo had security? When I saw him at the gala, there were no bodyguards. I should not have been able to get anywhere near him. By the time two of his security appeared, Leo could have already been killed several times over. Unknown armed men, which were not part of his security detail, also followed him."

Synn glances back at me and meets my eyes. Her gorgeous, joyful eyes are full of weariness and pain.

She has had enough.

That is it. My parents can wait.

"Mom, Dad, it is time you left. Essy needs to heal and cannot if she is being questioned and interrogated. She needs to sleep."

"We need to know what is happening, Declyn."

I have had enough. My parents have pushed me enough. "No. You need to leave. Go question Leo."

Chapter Sixteen

ESSY

I must have nodded off, because the next thing I know, my room is empty. The silence presses in, heavy and sterile, broken only by the faint hum of machines and the faint antiseptic tang in the air. Memories flood back, reminding me of what happened — the chaos, the gunfire, the pain. My chest and shoulder throb, radiating pulses that feel worse now than before, each beat reminding me I'm still alive.

At least Dekk had the sense to remove his parents from my room. I love them, but right now I need quiet. And honestly, I need my sister more than anyone.

A soft tapping at the door pulls me back. I glance up to see Laini standing there, worry etched across her face, her hand hovering near the doorframe like she's afraid to intrude.

"Hey, you. Is it okay for me to come in?" she whispers, sneaking a look over her shoulder before meeting my eyes.

I take it Dekk told everyone to leave me alone. As much as I love that man, I still need my sister.

With a smile, I croak, "Come on. Before Dekk sees you."

She slips inside with a playful grin, shutting the door behind her like she's sneaking contraband. She perches on the edge of my bed, her hand immediately finding its way to my belly. "How are the rug rats going?"

One babe pushes against her palm, and her face lights up, joy spilling across her features. "Hey there, little one. Behaving yourself in there?" Her voice is soft, affectionate, the kind of tone that makes my heart ache. The babe shifts, repositioning, and Laini's eyes sparkle.

She's going to be one proud aunty. I can already picture her spoiling them rotten, probably teaching them sarcasm before they can walk.

Her smile fades when her gaze meets mine. "You're lucky to be alive, Essy. You were hit twice. You could have been killed." Her voice trembles, then steadies. She glances to her right, nods, and smiles faintly. "Betsy is glad you and the babes are okay."

I glance around the room, realizing her ghost is here. Betsy has been part of Laini's life since she moved into Betsy house as a teenager. Betsy was murdered on her way home from work in the eighties. She was a respected surgeon, a highly sought-after specialist in her field. Word has it, her death had something to do with the Apolo Syndicate. Ghosty Betsy definitely comes with an interesting résumé. And apparently, she cares about my babies, too.

"Thanks, Betsy. I know you were there helping Laini that night. Thanks for keeping her safe."

Laini smiles, tilts her head down with a slight shake. "She says, 'Any time.'"

Yeah, I bet Betsy said more than that. My sister looks way too embarrassed.

Then Laini lifts her brow. "Have you contacted Mom and Dad?"

Shit. I shake my head slowly. They're going to panic when they hear I've been shot. I haven't even seen my cell. Hopefully it's safe.

"No. I haven't had time." My eyes flick to the door, half-expecting Dekk to walk in. Annoying man or not, I've missed him more than I realized. I squeeze Laini's hand. "You haven't contacted them?"

She shakes her head. She grabs the water cup, passes it to me. I sip, the cool slide down my throat heavenly. "I don't know where my cell is. Can you call them on yours and pass it to me?"

She nods, pulls out her phone. "Hey. I also snuck in here to give you a heads up. Two cops are downstairs. They want to speak to us. Especially you — bullet wounds attract attention." She sits back down, passes me her phone. Our parents' name lights up as it rings.

"Monkey hairy balls. I wondered how long it would take the PD to come sniffing. Hopefully we can stall them."

She nods. I tap hands-free. Mom's laugh fills the room, followed by her voice: "How are you, baby girl? Is everything okay?"

I glance at Laini. "Hello, Mom. I'm here with Laini."

"Essy?" Bugger. Panic already in her tone. "Is everything all right? Why are you using Laini's phone? Is she okay?"

Laini leans in. "I'm here, Mom." She smiles at me, rolls her eyes.

"Laini, what's going on?" My sister gives me the tell her look.

"Umm. Mom. I'm in the hospital."

"What? Why? How?" she rants.

"Mom, let me explain."

"You better start, young lady. Laini, why didn't you contact us before now?"

Laini's shoulders slump. Busted. For once, the perfect sister's in trouble. I'd feel smug if I wasn't half-dead.

"Mom. Listen. Laini came with me to an event my old client attended. Long story short, we were followed and ambushed. There was a shootout. Many shooters were killed."

"What? Who followed my girls?"

"That's what I'd like to know," I mumble, wondering if anyone snapped photos.

Laini clears her throat. "Um... Dekk pushed for photos when he arrived."

He what...? I knew I loved that man for a reason. I wiggle my fingers at Laini. Give me the pictures.

"Who is Dekk?" Mom demands.

"Ahh, Mom. You need to know a couple of things."

"Essynda, what is it? What are you hesitant to reveal?"

Laini smiles, nods for me to continue. I drag in a

breath. "Mom, you know how we haven't seen each other for three months or so."

"Yes, Essy. Your father and I have been wondering why you avoided our dinners."

"Well, Mom, I have joyous news. You and Dad will be grandparents." My eyelids droop, a yawn escapes.

"What?" Mom screeches. My eyes snap open. "Since when? Hang on. Since when have you had time to be in a relationship, let alone get pregnant?" Well, thanks a lot, Mom.

Before she continues, I cut in. "Mom, I'm married and expecting twins."

"Twins... Married?" Another yawn hits. My eyes flutter closed. I'm more worn out than I thought.

"Look, Mom. I'm calling because I need your and Dad's help. The local PD wants to question me. My husband and his twin are in danger." I sigh. "I was shot protecting my idiot brother-in-law. Don't worry. I'm okay, and so are the twins. But I need backup."

"Essynda, tell me where you are. Your father and I will be on the next plane," she says in her take-charge voice.

"Thanks, Mom. I'll let Laini fill you in. But I need to —" Another enormous yawn interrupts.

"Baby girl, you sound tired. Rest. We'll be there before you know it. Take care. We love you."

"Love you too, Mom," I mumble around another jaw-cracking yawn.

My family owns an old warehouse in the city. We've been turning it into apartments — one for me, one for Laini. Mine's still under construction, of course. Our parents have the penthouse, plenty of room for all of us, plus their PI office. Freelance work, occasional FBI cases. Time to use the high-rise with its 24/7 security.

Laini takes the phone, smiles, taps the screen, lifts it to her ear. Her eyes meet mine. "Get some sleep." She winks, smiles. "I'll speak with Mom and Dad." Then she walks out of my hospital room.

Chapter Seventeen

ESSY

*W*aiting is a pain in the butt. Being cooped up in this hospital for ten long, dull days just about did my head in. My only bit of entertainment was when the local PD questioned me several times. How do I answer their questions when I don't know the answers?

Wearing my own clothes again, I wait for the doctor to arrive for my final assessment and the last test results for the twins. Finally, a faint knock sounds before my hospital door opens, revealing my husband holding a drink tray with two cups and a bag of food.

Whenever Dekk spent any time in my room, it never lasted long. There was always something to interrupt his visit. I only wanted to snuggle into my husband's arms for twenty minutes. I don't know how the man crept under my skin and found his way to my heart. But I must admit to myself I do love him. I have for a long time.

As soon as his eyes meet mine, a smile transforms

his face. "Hey, Essy." His eyes search the room, most likely looking for the doctor. Not seeing anyone else, he continues, "Has the doctor arranged a time to drop by?"

Hairy monkey balls. The doctor should have been here an hour ago.

I shake my head. "He was meant to be here by now," I murmur and rub my belly. Have I said I hate hospitals?

"Essy." Dekk places his items on the side table. "We need to talk." I lift my brow and wait for him to finish. "My parents want us to stay with them until whoever is after my family is stopped or apprehended."

Wow, that is interesting. Dekk's words have my eyebrows raised. I don't think so, husband! His parents dislike me. Even under normal circumstances, I would not stay under their roof. I'm relieved Dekk has arrived before anyone else in the family today. Finally, some privacy.

With the police investigation and the hospital staff constantly coming and going, my parents took charge of my security. So there's been no privacy for us to discuss anything.

"I am glad you are here." I smile. Well, I am glad. I am over being stuck in this stupid, smelly room. "We should stay with my parents instead."

"What do you mean, your parents?" His frown is comical. Let's see if I can convince him.

"Dekk, I asked my parents to assist and follow up on a few things, especially on the hitmen from the ambush."

"What are you saying?" he says with his hands

planted firmly on his hips. I can see he is not impressed with my suggestion.

"Here, help me up."

Dekk steps forward and reaches out for my good arm. I nod and attempt to stand. His hands reach for my hips when I lose my balance. With one arm in a sling, it will take me longer to adjust to my newly injured situation. Something I am definitely not used to.

The heat of Dekk's hands radiates through my clothing, sending sweet chills through my body — carnal sensations only he can do. I glance at his eyes and notice they are focused on my lips. Without thinking, I automatically brush my tongue slowly along them.

Dekk gulps, and I feel his grip on my hips intensify. "Essy, do you have any idea what you do to me?" he whispers. I glance at his lips, then back at his eyes, and see they are heated with passion.

Before I can reply, the warmth of his lips brushes my own twice. The soft touch of his lips evokes feelings I have kept locked away. Maybe a little too long. He presses against me and repeats his actions, sending my hormones into overdrive. Finally, my defenses crumble, and I return his kiss, taking command.

Passion takes hold as our lips fuse in a kiss I have missed. Hands caress, touching, squeezing, and stroking one another through our clothing. We are hungry and eager for more of each other as our lips part enough, allowing our tongues to duel for dominance. I hear growling and am not sure if it is him or me. He slides his tongue along mine until I thrust mine back into his mouth, and he takes hold of it and sucks. Heat increases in my belly and lower. I attempt to pull away long enough so I can breathe, only for Dekk to bring my body against his. I feel one of his hands slide around to my butt, squeezing and massaging my globe before his entire hand covers my butt cheek, urging my body closer to his, feeling his hard length press against me.

The chemistry between us has always been off the charts. How I kept myself away from Dekk, I'll never know. When I was his personal bodyguard, he broke my three rules all those months ago. The sexy man crept into my heart and soul and activated my inner seductress. Something I never knew I had, let alone know how to use, but my husband released her. I soon discovered I could seduce my sexy husband in ways I would never have imagined doing to any other man.

Heat increases between my thighs, turning my underwear wet. I don't know if it is my pregnancy hormones, but my husband has flicked my seductress switch. I want him naked and on my bed — now!

With my free hand, I work my way between us and under his sweater and t-shirt. Wow. My husband has gained more of that gorgeous toned muscle I enjoy so much, and I begin my journey down to the waistband of his dress pants.

It does not take me long to have the button and zip undone. Yes. My treasure is nearly in my hand. As I slide my hand into his underwear, a firm knock sounds against my hospital door, causing us to pause. We pull apart enough to feel our panting breath racing against one another's heated, wet, swollen lips and gently lean our foreheads together.

Reality hits, reminding me we are still in the hospital.

Monkey hairy balls.

Who in the world has shit timing!

Dekk angles his head slightly and kisses my lips again. "Raincheck, Wife," he whispers against my lips.

"Raincheck, Husband," I whisper back with a smile.

I pull away and carefully sit back down on the bed, and Dekk turns towards the window and casually fixes his pants. Damn, it's been far too long since I have had the pleasure of his body.

I turn enough and face the door and watch it slowly open.

The doctor I had been patiently waiting for had finally arrived, and he must have seen Dekk and me kissing by the look on his face. It is only a matter of seconds before his face changes to his doctor's face once more.

"Ms. Bianchi."

"Mrs. Bianchi," I reply.

I watch the doctor glance at Dekk before turning back to me. "Yes. Mrs. Bianchi. The results for the babes show they are healthy and growing. However, your blood pressure has been constantly on the higher side, which is not a good sign. You'll require rest. No stress for at least two weeks, maybe longer."

I can't sit around all day, let alone for two weeks. I have criminals to apprehend and send to jail.

"There must be some mistake. Surely I don't need to laze about for two weeks?"

Dekk is back by my side. He reaches for my hand and gives it a firm squeeze.

"Mrs. Bianchi, there are no ifs or buts. Gestational hypertension can lead to Preeclampsia. It is no joking matter. To prioritize your safety, it is necessary for you to rest. If your blood pressure rises, both you and your twins will be at risk."

The doctor's words race through my mind. Gestational hypertension. Preeclampsia. Reality hits. I didn't realize I was being selfish. I can't lose my precious boys.

The sting of tears makes themselves known in my eyes. I glance up and see the concern in Dekk's.

"Essy, you need to listen to the doctor. I do not want to lose you or the twins." The tone in his voice cracks through my heart.

A tear escapes and rolls down my cheek. Monkey hairy balls. Damn, these hormones.

Dekk places his other hand on my belly. Movement from within zeros in on Dekk's hand, bringing a smile to his face. "Hey, little one," he croons. His hand makes circular motions around my belly. He glances up at my face with a huge smile and love in his eyes. "Essy. Okay. We will stay with your parents. Plus, they will have a better chance of controlling you than me. You know I have a hard time saying no to you."

Yes, I know he has trouble saying no to me. I have used that scenario to my advantage many times. But, realistically, I am relieved he has agreed to go to my parents. We will be safe under their protection.

$\mathcal{M}$y beautiful wife might think she has out-smarted me — even though she has a habit of it. I know the sexy woman will be safer under her family's protection.

Now we know Synn will remain at the hospital for several more days, we should take advantage of the alone time before anyone else interrupts us. But first, I need to explain where I was the night of my brother's BS engagement party.

Synn beats me to it and speaks before I even have a chance. "I think you should sit down," she advised, her tone filled with concern. "There is something you need to know," she said, her words hanging in the air like a heavy secret. Uh-oh.

"Know what?" keeping my voice calm. I wonder if it has something to do with my brother.

Synn pats the bed, encouraging me to sit down beside her. She waits until I place my butt on the bed before she makes a sound. "Honey, I discovered something about your uncle."

My uncle. Not my brother! I remain silent, my brows furrowing in confusion. Apart from being dead, there isn't much else to know about my uncle.

"Did your father ever mention his brother had a girlfriend before he died?" I shake my head, unsure where Synn is going with her question. "I have since discovered your uncle and his girlfriend named Melissa, also had a child."

Whoa, now that is news. "What? When? Who…"

"Your cousin is about the same age as you and Leo."

A cousin. I have a cousin! Shocked is an understatement for how I'm feeling. I stand and begin walking back and forth, shaking my head in disbelief. "How in the world did I end up with a cousin I never knew I had?" I pause and glance over my shoulder at Synn. "My father mentioned nothing about my uncle's girlfriend or child."

"Dekk, you need to speak with your father and Leo. Your aunt could be behind the attacks." Now that has me turning towards her. My aunt!

Huh? "What? Why?"

"What would you do if your mother had to raise you and Leo without your father? How would she handle raising a child without the benefits of the family name and money? Abandoned."

I sit back down to contemplate her words.

"Okay, Synn. I understand where you are coming from."

I face Synn, meeting her eyes, and watch her sharp

eyebrow rise. "Do you? Because a woman scorned can be dangerous."

Not sure what to feel, my shoulders sag. "Okay, Essy, I believe you." As young adults growing up, Leo and I had left our hook-ups or ex-girlfriends for the staff to deal with, not giving the women a second thought. I am glad I grew up and faced responsibilities. Not like my twin, who does not care. It might be time to bring Synn up on the little investigation on the pier. "I think it is time I updated you about the meeting on the wharf the other night."

"What meeting?" she questions. I can see her brain is busy at work, and she is not happy with her thoughts. She turns her face toward me and asks, "Is that why you were not with Leo?"

"Look, Essy, since our work arrangement ended all those months ago, Leo and I started receiving death threats about a month later."

Her eyes widen, and she shakes her head. "Why didn't you contact me?"

"Essy, our marriage was in name only. You were busy with your work, as I was busy with mine. I know how passionate you are when you're working on a case. You said you had a new contract for two months." Which meant — do not contact me. I'm busy!

She gives me an annoyed look. "Dekk, that is no excuse. You're still my husband. If you required my help and protection..." She takes a deep breath to calm herself. "Okay, explain to me. What were you doing on the wharf?"

Her brow is prominent again. She waits patiently for me to begin.

"Essy, I have been trying to discover who is behind the threats."

"Well, have you discovered who it is?"

Uh-oh. I avoid meeting her eyes and glance down and mumble. "Umm. I thought... I, um, discovered the Apolo Syndicate."

"You what?" she screeches and attempts to get up. But instead, she lands back down on her delicious butt. "Do you realize who the Apolo Syndicate is?"

I place my hand against her shoulder, keeping her upright. Crazy feelings fleet up through my fingers, arm, and straight to my groin.

"Yes, Essy. I know exactly who the Apolo Syndicate is and what they are capable of." Her eyes meet mine with a questioning look. "I don't think they are the actual ones after us. I think they are only guns for hire."

"What would make you say that?" She reaches for my hand, wrapping her fingers around mine. "Did you take any pictures?"

"Ahh, my feisty wife." I smile at my gorgeous love. "I filmed the meeting."

She shakes her head at my words. "So, my sneaky husband, where is this footage right now?" she casually asks with a straight face.

"Before you get too excited, I gave your parents a copy." I thought it best to give them the heads-up while Synn has been out of action. "Now, do you have your cell handy?" I request with a smile.

*S*ynn had explained her investigation into my family. Digging deeper for more medical information for our twins, she discovered some information regarding my uncle's name linked to a babe born after his death — a son. He is believed to have belonged to my uncle's girlfriend.

Did my father know about this woman?

My father made it seem like his brother died because of the curse.

My lovely wife and I made the transition to her parent's building and slept in separate guest bedrooms. Her parents have agreed to take over the research of my deceased uncle's girlfriend and the mysterious woman's child and my video footage down at the wharf.

Since leaving the hospital, my brother received another death threat, then three days later, my father received one, discovering it on his home office desk. Today, my mother demanded something to be done regarding their safety. My father agreed to stay under the protection of Synn's family. Smart man. Or cunning, to use my wife and her family and let someone else foot the bill.

*I*n my in-laws' large formal lounge area, I attempt to find a comfortable position and shuffle on a large, soft leather armchair. Thankfully, security buzzed a couple of minutes ago to inform me my parents and brother were on their way up. A knock on the door had me turning my head.

About time.

My parents and Leo were due to arrive over an hour ago.

Thank goodness Synn is taking her nap. She doesn't need the added stress.

Unease fills me as I stand by the door. I hate confrontation with my parents. The big question is, how much does my mother know about the family curse and my father's brother? I suppose there is only one way to find out.

My white-knuckled fingers are wrapped tightly around the door handle, and I'm hesitant to open the door. Second thoughts rush through my mind. Is it too late to change my mind?

You can do this. Just open the door like a grown-up.

Straightening my shoulders and putting on a fake smile, I gather the courage to open the door. The first thing that catches my attention is the intense glare from my parents, with my irritating brother standing beside them, all dressed in their finest attire. Despite knowing I would likely regret it, I reluctantly step back, allowing them to enter as their presence fills the room with a mixture of anticipation and apprehension.

In their typical fashion, they nonchalantly left their luggage by the door. Witnessing the selfishness of my own family, all I can do is shake my head in disappointment — their first mistake. There is absolutely no chance that they will receive royal treatment and be waited on with every need catered to.

With a straight face, I say, "Don't forget your luggage. And shut the door behind you." And walk towards the formal lounge area.

With many huffs and foul language coming from under their breaths, my parents, and brother pick up their luggage, and dump it inside the foyer, and close the door.

Three sets of footsteps soon follow.

"Declyn, what is going on?" my father demands.

I eye my brother, determining what he knows. He shakes his head and sits down on one lounge. My mother follows suit and eyes the room before staring at me.

I take in a deep breath and watch all three of them.

"Thank you for coming. Your rooms are ready for your stay." I look from one parent to the other, then to Leo. "My wife has come across some Intel, which affects all of us. However, she also clearly stated that we will be safer here under her parents' security protocols."

"What, Intel, Declyn?" my father demands.

I indicate for Father to sit, and I follow suit in the opposite armchair. Here goes...

"Dad, what do you remember about your twin brother's girlfriend?"

Dad glances towards Mom with a questionable look,

then back at me. "No, I don't remember Zaiden having a girlfriend before his death. As far as I am aware, he was single. Why?" Great. My father's face changes. A tell when he is lying.

"Uncle Zaiden did indeed have a girlfriend before his death. A pregnant girlfriend," I say with a straight face.

I watch Leo from the corner of my eye and turn to face him. I can see the question he wants to ask with a raised eyebrow. He wants to know if what I am saying is the truth. I nod and glance back at our father.

"How do you know if he had a pregnant girlfriend? Look, your uncle Zaiden and mother had been dating before we met. Once your mother met me, we only had eyes for one another. Your uncle disagreed with my relationship with your mother, but he had to adjust to the knowledge his ex-girlfriend was now my girlfriend, then my wife."

I glance toward Leo. He found it difficult to ascertain the nature of my bond with Synn. Throughout our lives, he was the one who always had a magnetic charm that attracted the girls. Women were drawn to him, and he had a knack for seducing them into his bed. Yet, when Synn entered our lives, he took offense to her lack of interest in his charisma or BS. It was hard to fathom how Synn, an enchanting and gorgeous woman, could have chosen me over my own brother, but she did.

"Essy explained everything to me. She was researching the medical history for our twins. She came across more than she had bargained for as she looked into our family history."

My father pushes to his feet and walks towards the hallway before stopping and returning to his seat. "I think your wife overstepped the mark and stepped into our family business without permission," my father states.

I stare Dad in the eye. "Dad, Essy knows about the problem the men in our family have."

"What men problem?" my mother demands. She scowls and looks to Dad, me, Leo, and back to Dad. "What am I not being told?" She halfway stands, then sits back with my father's hand firmly planted on her shoulder.

Leo and I glanced toward Mom before looking back at Dad. Would my father deceive his own brother to make sure he would live while his brother died? I meet Leo's eyes, and I can see he thinks the same thing I am. I don't know if I want to know if my father is a piece of scum or not, who only cares about himself and not his twin.

Even though my twin is a pain in my ass, I placed his life equal to my own. My sexy wife had agreed to save us. She saved us both. I wonder if my father had asked my mother. Would she have approved and helped save them both? Somehow, the way my mother acts prudish, I don't think she would allow two men to touch her simultaneously.

*W*asted time is all I can say. There are no words... I'm disappointed with my father. It does not take a genius to realize that Father mentioned nothing regarding the family curse to our mother, even though she deserved to know.

Right now, I do not want to speak with the man. Years ago, I could trust him. A man to admire in business. Once again, he's confirmed he's nothing but a heartless and careless human who only gives a fuck about himself and his family name. My father tripped up. I know for a fact he is lying. I wonder what else the man has lied to us about and what other family secrets he's kept from us.

It's time to speak with Synn regarding the mystery woman named Melissa, who was once part of my uncle's world.

Where is this woman, and who is she? And most of all, to discover who is behind the threats.

Chapter Nineteen

ESSY

*a*m I dreaming?

I wake to warm, firm lips sweeping along my naked neck, sending sensual tingles through my body and straight to my core, especially when said lips reach that secret spot right by my ear. Thanks to his signature cologne, I know accurately whose lips are causing my body to fill with need. It is the same sexy scent I gave my husband on his birthday. However, I know his twin's lips feel completely different against my flesh.

Declyn requested we sleep in separate guest rooms when we first arrived here. I had initially been annoyed with him. Once he explained, he would be coming and going at all hours with his business and the family business. He felt I would not rest, sleep, or heal. So, thanks to Dekk's thoughtfulness, I've managed to have a night of uninterrupted sleep and rest for several days, and I'm feeling better.

"Hmmm. If you are going to tempt a girl, you better

be naked," I purr as I turn my head enough and meet his sensual lips with mine.

I have waited too long to be intimate with my husband.

Finally. Right here. Right now.

We have the chance to make love. Something we have been denied since our brief honeymoon. From his hard length nudging me, I know he's interested.

Fast thoughts race through my mind. Does Dekk wish to remain married to me? Is he willing to turn this marriage of convenience into the real thing? More importantly — is he ready to love the twins and me?

My doubts disappear as our kiss heats, and the pressure between my legs is ready to explode. I maneuver enough to face my sexy naked husband and push my tongue into his mouth. Our tongues duel in a battle for dominance as I set my leg up and over his thighs, turning Dekk onto his back.

With my knees under me, I push up with my hand, careful not to place too much pressure on my injured shoulder. I rub my heated core over his hardening length, enticing our bodies.

Requiring air, I pull back enough to breathe, filling my lungs, as I sit up enough to maneuver his mushroom-shaped head between my thighs, coating him in my lubricant. Then I push down, guiding him inside my body on the next swivel of my hips, slowly sinking down.

We both groan in pleasure. His large intrusion gradually filled and stretched me just the right way, touching me in all the right places. How I have missed our time together, especially him. Dekk is the only man who can satisfy my body's needs. I open my eyelids and see the desire radiating from Dekk's eyes, and, for once, it does not scare me. I continue to lift and slowly sink back down along Dekk's length until I can fit him all in and sit there, allowing my body to adjust to his long, wide, pulsing girth.

His fingers dig into my hips and hold me in place. I can tell he is holding himself back — waiting. "Synn, I need to know. Can the babies become injured? I don't want to hurt them or you," he says between clenched teeth.

There he goes again. I don't think he realizes he calls me Synn. The man has moaned, whispered and also spoke that name in his sleep. I slide along his length with another sensual moan. "Honey, it is safe. Now, fuck me. It has been far too long," I manage to say before rolling to my side. Dekk lifts my top leg higher and thrusts deep and hard.

With a groan of his own, Dekk speeds up his thrusts. His hand grabs purchase on my ass, keeps me in place, and repeatedly thrusts fast. Finally, he releases my butt and spreads out over my body, placing his hand beside my head, keeping his weight away from my belly, and allowing me to swivel my hips to encourage him in deeper. He caresses and touches my sensual zones from his new position, lighting up my tightening core.

Before I can warn him, my core pulses, and my legs begin to shake. My inner muscles squeeze tight and flutter around his solid length, milking him. My pants of ecstasy echo around the room. Dekk loudly grunts his release and thrusts a couple more times, lodging himself as deep as possible before collapsing back against the bed, keeping our lower bodies joined.

I turn my head and lean into Dekk's body, our breathing, and hearts racing in sync, placing a kiss on his chest. He wraps one arm around me, holding me against his body.

The touch of his lips on my forehead is soft and lingering, sending a wave of comfort through me. I can sense his thoughts brewing in the silence. It's possible that he was overthinking and making things more complicated than they needed to be. I hope he does not have any second thoughts about making love to me.

"I love you, Synn." Huh? My breath stalls in my throat.

Did he just say what I think I just heard? I thought he was regretting what we did.

"Never forget that," he pants. "I should have said it all those months ago. But...I didn't want to scare you." He kisses my head again. Okay... Should I allow hope to fill me? But he just confessed his love for me. He loves me. My pulse speeds up. He really loves me! "I never want us to be separated again." He doesn't want to be separated? What does that mean, exactly? "I have missed you so much." He brushes his lips against my forehead with little butterfly kisses. "Breathe, Essy." He squeezes me tighter. Oh, bugger. I forgot I was holding my breath. I take in a sharp breath, filling my lungs.

Can I allow myself to believe him?

Am I dreaming?

"If you didn't understand me, I said, I. Love. You."
Oh, my.

He loves me!

These are the sweetest words any woman wants to hear from her man.

"I have missed you, too," I whisper. Am I brave enough to say it back? It's time to face facts. I do love this man. I always have. He needs to hear me say those three little words. Come on, Essy, you can do it.

Our eyes meet. "Dekk, I love you so much." I squeeze his arm. "It hurt to be parted from you."

I hear Dekk sigh. "Thank the universe. I was afraid of saying anything. I didn't want to scare you." He gives me another squeeze. "And I completely agree. It hurt as if my heart had been ripped out of my chest and stopped beating, unable to see your beautiful face." He kisses my head again and places his hand on my belly. "I have missed so much. Tell me everything from when you discovered you were pregnant. What was going through your mind? Everything."

With a lifted brow, I ask, "Before we get too far ahead of ourselves are you going to explain the name you call me — Synn."

His eyes widen then his lips twitch.

"Well...I usually call you Synn in my head. As in — your sin in body, sin in nature, and sin in my bed." His eyes meet mine. "Essy, I love you and you are the Synn of my heart and soul. My forever."

My eyes mist and all I can do is nod.

Wrapped in one another's arms, we lay back in the bed and talked, including the full version of the so-called family curse. After all this time, we finally revealed our thoughts and feelings, what we should have said from the beginning, covering everything that had happened since our short honeymoon. We made love, again and again, catching up for lost time, and fell asleep exhausted, tangled in each other's arms.

The sound of knocking wakes me from a peaceful sleep. I go to sit up, only to discover an arm wrapped over my waist and curved around my belly.

Dekk. A smile forms, and I turn my head enough and kiss his shoulder.

"Hey. There is someone at the door," I whisper.

I feel Dekk tighten his hold and snuggle into my back and neck.

"Maybe if we pretend we cannot hear them, they will go away?" Wishful thinking on Dekk's part until he thrusts his hips. We both release a groan of pleasure. His hard length lets me know he is fully embedded within me. He swivels his hips, and, with another thrust, his flesh glides back and forth, enticing my body.

I was lost in mind-blowing pleasure with my husband until the knocking sound interrupted my sexual bliss, annoying my senses.

"Dekk, I don't think they are going away," I pant.

He slides his flesh a couple more times between my

thighs before groaning in frustration. He stops. He lifts his head enough and calls out, "Who is it?" before placing another kiss along my shoulder, making his way up my neck, and gently thrusting inside me again.

"Declyn, we need to talk," Leo yells through the door. Damn it.

The next thing I hear is the door handle moving about. By its sounds, Dekk locked my door before coming to bed. Thank goodness.

"Declyn, open the bloody door now," Leo demands.

Finally, I am in bed wrapped in my husband's arms, waking up and making love, and my annoying brother-in-law is banging on the door. "No, Leo. Go away. We are sleeping," I yell out.

"Sorry, Sweets, but I need to speak with my brother."

With his front plastered to my back and fully embedded between my thighs. Dekk angrily says, "What about, Leo? Can't it wait?"

The door handle rattles again. "No. Now, let me in."

Dekk swears under his breath towards his brother. He pulls his body from mine, leaving me feeling empty. He picks up his pants from the floor and forces his feet in them until he stands tall, leaving his button undone. Poor guy, he's sporting a raging hard-on, and it looks painful. Dekk stomps over to the door, flick the locks and opens it to a scowling Leo. Thankfully, I pulled the sheet up to cover my body before Dekk opened the door.

"This better be important, Leo. My wife was sleeping," Dekk rants at his brother.

Leo strides in, glancing at his brother, noticing Dekk's painful bulge with the shiny head pocking out from his pants, smiles, turns, and stares at me, probably visualizing what I look like under the sheet, knowing full well what we had been doing before he interrupted.

"Hurry up, Leo. What is it you want to say?" Dekk closes the door and sits beside me on the bed, wrapping me in his arms and pressing a kiss to my naked shoulder.

Leo watches Dekk and is not amused. Ha. Jealous much, Leo? "Dad is serious about having your marriage annulled."

What the fuck. My father-in-law can't do that!

"Leo, we both know that will not happen. I am legally married to Essynda."

"Dad does not care. He wants you to marry Lucille Chambers. He will not stop until he makes sure it happens."

Dekk gives Leo a strange look. Shake's his head, changing his mind at whatever he was thinking. "Have you spoken to Dad about our uncle? Did you mention anything about the family curse?" Dekk demands.

With a shake of his head, Leo looks away. Bloody gutless wonder. He always had Dekk fight his battles and get him out of trouble.

"Leo, we have more important matters to deal with than your father's business dealings. Our lives are in danger. Whoever threatens us must be found and stopped," I declare, unhappy with Leo's presence.

"Look, Sweets, the family dealings are important."

I shake my head. "Leo, grow a set of balls. Your father needs to learn. His son has his own life. Which includes a wife and soon-to-be children in a few more months."

"Sweets, our father is determined to end your marriage. He only sees dollar signs, and marriage between Dekka and Lucille would make that happen."

I seethe, between clenched teeth, "Leo, your father does not know just how wealthy my family is, let alone how successful I am." Sucking in a breath, I continue. "Plus, I would not care if Dekk had no money. I have enough for the two of us. Well, soon to be four!"

"It does not matter, Sweets. Our father is not making any money from your union with Dekka."

"Look, boys, no offense, but your father can fuck off. I have no time for his BS." I turn and glance at the bedside table and read the time. Hairy monkey balls. Lunch. "Leo, go back to your room and get changed. Lunch will be served in the formal dining room in less than half an hour. We'll meet you."

I turn and look at Dekk and point my head to his brother, then the door. Dekk releases me from his firm hold and moves off the bed.

"Come on, bro. It's time to leave." Dekk encourages Leo to the door. "As Essy said, you need to return to your room," came the command. We will see you soon."

In one swift motion, Dekk shoves his brother out the door and slams it shut, the sound of the lock clicking follows. Turning around with a mischievous grin, my husband's heated gaze lands on me. "Right. Where were we?" He quickly moves forward and jumps onto the bed, causing me to squeal like a little girl. "Synn, you have been a dirty girl, and it is time for me to make sure you are clean," he laughs as his hands grip the sheets.

With a mixture of laughter and excitement, I shake my head as he playfully rips the bedsheet away, sending a delightful chill down my exposed body, and then carries me effortlessly into the bathroom.

Wrapping my legs around my husband's waist, I let out a surprised gasp as my back meets the icy touch of the bathroom tiles. The cascading water quickly warms my body, along with the comforting heat radiating from Dekk. Even though Declyn's meticulous cleaning routine caused us to be late for lunch, I can honestly say that I savored every second of it. Sorry. Not sorry.

Chapter Twenty
ESSY

*E*ven ten days later, I am still asking myself how I allowed Leo and his father to convince us to attend the dinner function on the upper private floor overlooking the water at Angelina's on Staten Island.

My father's temper was on the verge of exploding when I relayed Dekk's father's demands. I swear steam was escaping out of his ears.

"Essy, it is far too dangerous. There is no security. You will be sitting ducks," my father explains.

I was well aware of the risks and took the time to thoroughly explain them to Dekk. Despite his father's insistence, he can also come across as rude, unreasonable, and a complete jackass.

"Daddy, I know. I will be armed." My lips twitch, and my eyebrow lifts. Back-up is a must. "I will take Jeffery and Sammy, plus one of your drivers, if you allow it. I want Dekk and me to have as much security as we can get away with." The jackass of a father-in-law is adamant that my marriage will be annulled. The question is... what does he have in mind? "I do not trust my father-in-law. He is determined to end my marriage with Dekk."

"He's what?" my father says, his voice rising, and I can see his anger increasing. "Does he believe that my little girl is not good enough to be part of his family... well, the fool has shown his inability to meet my expectations. He is not good enough in any capacity for my little girl and our family." My heart fills with joy — hearing my father say my father-in-law is not good enough for me. I watch him walk back and forth, stop and face me. "Essy, carry extra ammunition. Inform your husband that he will also carry a gun. Go, and finish getting ready, and I'll have my men downstairs waiting to drive you to the Italian restaurant in twenty minutes."

Awkwardly, I stand before my dad and, with a bit of effort, wrap my good arm around him, feeling the warmth of his embrace. "Thank you, Daddy. I love you."

"I know, pumpkin. Your mother and I love you, too. Now, go. Get ready and wear the black arm sling. It has an inbuilt holder for your gun."

Just as I go to open the door, I hear my father on the phone arranging for my security. My parents are planning to be there.

*B*efore leaving for the dinner event, I had a private conversation with Dekk, ensuring that he had a loaded handgun he was proficient in handling. We also discussed the conversation I had with my father, ensuring he had a thorough understanding of how we were to proceed. With a shake of his head, my husband watched as I secured my loaded gun with its attached silencer in the specialized holder of my arm sling, and extra ammo in my jacket pocket.

Against his parents' wishes, Leo annoyingly joins us in the back of our family town car.

Dekk turns to his brother and asks, "What's the real reason we're having dinner at Angelina's?" He shakes his head and looks out the window, mumbling, "Why do I feel there will be other people in attendance?"

As if he didn't hear Dekk mumble the last question, Leo says, "You know what Dad's like. I overheard him mention that Caroline would be there with her parents. Also, there will be a few others. I am not sure who they are."

I watch Leo quickly glance towards me and then back to Dekk. The guy is full of BS. He knows exactly who will be there.

"Leo, don't bullshit me. You are well aware of the exact individuals that father has invited. Just say it, so we can at least prepare for the shit show our parents have planned for us tonight," Dekk demands, annoyance filling his words.

Once again, Leo glances in my direction. What is he hiding?

I cannot help myself. I have to say something, "Just tell us, Leo. Stop playing around and grow some balls, will ya."

His shoulders slump, and he sighs in defeat. "Okay. Okay. Dad has arranged for this dinner to be a business meeting. Eric Chambers will be there with his wife Susan and daughter Lucille."

You have to be bloody kidding me... I squeeze Dekk's hand before he lifts our entwined hands and kisses the back of mine. I meet his eyes with my own and see love in his dark blue depths.

With Leo and Dekk being identical twins, right down to their eye coloring, I've always preferred Dekk. His attitude was different towards most things from that of his brother. Plus, he is more caring and not selfish.

Plus, Dekk is wearing his wedding band I had placed on his finger months ago and the diamond stud earring I slipped into the piercing on his left ear, which he proudly wears. My father had also made it into a high-tech tracker in case anyone attempted to kidnap him. I am wearing the matching stud high on the helix in my ear.

Tonight I am wearing a pair of thigh-high leather black boots, which also contain a small handgun in one and a throwing knife in the other. A blue form-fitting maternity dress, which reaches just past my knees, showcases my baby bulge and breasts — a thigh-length black evening jacket to finish my look.

My father suggested, well, demanded for me to wear the gorgeous sapphire necklace adorned with multiple stones around my neck. The centerpiece contains gold swirls with an encrusted diamond pendant, which encases a hidden micro camera with audio. Something I can turn on and off for those private moments in my life — nothing more embarrassing than when you go to the bathroom to relieve yourself and forget you are being listened to. Having an extra set of eyes with me provides added security.

I ensure the necklace is sitting correctly and gently press the activate button to record. My father made sure I wore a small earpiece to keep in contact with my parents, which was hard to see and detect.

Within seconds, my father's firm tones quietly fill my ear. "Testing. Lift your hand in front of you and check your nails."

My father's words just about have me laughing. Since when do I check my nails? Dekk will wonder what I am up to.

I check my nails to indicate I can hear my father.

"Thanks, baby girl. We have audio and visual. All systems are a go," my father says in my earpiece.

I smile and glance at Dekk. He catches me looking at him, and he lifts my hand once again and kisses the back of it. I wink and give him another smile before turning and looking Leo in the eye.

"Well, Leo, are you going to finish filling us in? I know there has to be more to your father's plans for tonight," I demand, keeping my voice level and polite.

"Umm. I think it would be wise for you to stick together. I would not put it past Father to separate the two of you and have Dekka sitting next to Lucille."

I feel Dekk flinch at Leo's words. So my lowlife

father-in-law wants to play dirty. I squeeze my husband's hand and say, "Hmm. We might have to arrange for a special toast to celebrate our nuptials and the twins. What do you say, Dekk?"

He smiles and leans over and kisses the corner of my mouth. The heat of his lips encourages me to turn my head and continue our sensual kiss, which quickly turns into a very steamy kiss. Leo coughs, and my father's voice in my ear grabs my attention. "Essy, you are nearly there. Get ready."

I pull back from my husband's delicious lips and smile. "Rain check?"

Dekk smiles back and nods. "Definitely, yes, we will. Raincheck." He leans forward and captures my lips in a quick kiss, sending another surge of lust through me.

"Okay, guys. We have arrived. Can you at least behave for half an hour?" Leo grumbles.

Dekk and I look at one another, smile, and shake our heads. "Nope. If I want to kiss my beautiful wife, brother, I will. Now come on. Let's get this fake dinner started."

With all our kissing, I did not feel the car come to a stop. The driver is already out and opening the door for me to get out first. He carefully assists me to my feet, and Dekk quickly gets out and wraps his arm around me. Leo casually slides out and stands beside his brother. I noticed that the driver, aka Davies, one of my father's security members, glanced around to ensure it was clear. He nods at me, and I nod back.

Dekk threads our arms together, and we make our way toward the multi-story building with all the fancy columns. As I step on the front steps, tingles begin along my spine.

Hairy monkey balls.

It would have been nice to have dinner without drama or issues with my husband.

Dekk slows our steps and whispers in my ear, "What is it, Synn? You have that look."

I smile, press my lips to his, and reply, "Tingles have started."

"Well, shit," Dekk says, and Leo mumbles something under his breath.

Chapter Twenty-One

DEKK

*I*f I'm not mistaken, the driver is one of my in-laws' security people, since he just gave Synn the heads-up. I hope that means the area is clear. With her injured shoulder strapped in a sling — her small handgun tucked neatly inside, because of course my wife is forever armed — I wrap my arm around her good side to keep her steady.

My beautiful wife. Always armed, always ready.

We head for the front reception at Angelina's.

Leo moves to my other side as we climb the steps. A woman in a tailored suit approaches, name tag pinned to her chest, smile plastered on her face.

I read her badge. "Hello, Ebony. We're here for dinner under the reservation name Bianchi."

She glances at the three of us, her eyes settling on my wife with a frown. "Hello, I'll be your hostess this evening. And your names?"

"Declyn and Essynda Bianchi, and my brother, Leo Bianchi."

Ebony frowns again. "I'm sorry. I don't remember seeing the name Essynda Bianchi."

"Well, Ebony, I suggest you make sure there's a setting for my wife," I grit out. Damn my parents. "Now, show us where this inappropriate family dinner will be held."

She frowns once more, then forces a smile. "Certainly. This way."

We follow her through the foyer, up a flight of stairs, along a corridor lined with doors, until we reach an elegant dining room. Balcony doors stand open, revealing a water view. The table is set for seven. My parents aren't here yet. Leo mutters under his breath — we all hear it — my parents didn't plan a place for my wife. Typical. At least we can rearrange before they arrive.

I walk Synn to the table and sit her in my seat. The place card beside me reads Lillian. I scoop up all the cards and hand them to Ebony.

"This is not good enough. Add another setting before the guests arrive. They won't be happy if they discover you're short." I nod, dismissing her.

I sit next to Synn. Leo takes the other side. A server approaches, smile wide, name tag catching the light.

"David," I read. Hopefully this one's competent. "A bottle of sparkling water, please."

Leo lifts his head. "Beer."

I turn to Synn, already knowing she wants something other than water.

"Orange juice. Then a glass of lemonade, please," she says with a smile.

"Make that two," I add. With Synn pregnant, I won't touch alcohol. And with her tingles, we need clear heads.

David eyes her, then nods. "Very well. I'll bring your drinks directly."

Ebony returns with staff, one pushing a cart of plates, one carrying a chair. They quickly rearrange the table. Ebony meets my eyes; I nod thanks. She leaves.

We survey the room.

Quietly, I ask, "So, what do you think of this place so far?"

Synn raises a brow, smiling faintly. She'd rather be anywhere else. Leo, meanwhile, is eyeing Ebony like she's dessert.

Synn notices, elbows him.

"Ow." He rubs his side. "What was that for?"

"Oh, I don't know... maybe because your fiancée will be here any minute," Synn spits. "Behave for once, Leo. Keep your head clear, be polite, stay alert."

"Me? Why do I have to be polite?" he grumbles as David returns with drinks.

"Here you go, folks." He sets Leo's beer down, places sparkling water between Synn and me, then her orange juice and lemonade, then mine.

"Thank you, David," I nod.

He smiles. "Anything else? Or will you wait for the other guests?"

"That's all for now."

He heads back to Ebony, speaking quietly with her.

I lift my glass with Synn and Leo. We tap glasses. "Cheers."

Anxiety coils in my gut as the other guests arrive through the public doorway. Great. Showtime.

J smile at Synn. She leans into me. We kiss, my hand resting on her baby bulge. Movement under my palm makes me pause, watching my hand rise and fall with the twins' kicks.

"Hey, little one. Behave for your mother," I murmur. The sound of guests shuffling to their seats reaches my ears, but I don't care. Let them stare. I'm here with my wife, and no one — not my father, not his scheming friends, not even Leo's ridiculous fiancée — will stop me from kissing her. So I do. I tilt her chin, press my lips to hers again, deliberately, unapologetically, because she's mine and I want the whole damn room to know it.

"Really, Declyn!" my father growls. "What do you think you're doing with that woman?"

I turn to him. "Seriously, Dad... if I want to kiss my pregnant wife, whom I love, I will." My voice carries louder than intended. I lift my glass, my wedding band catching the light.

The room freezes. Eyes lock on my hand. Lucille's mouth drops open, eyes wide. The older couple beside her scowl at my father.

"Bianchi, what is going on? Why is your son claiming he's married when four weeks ago he wasn't?"

Before my father can speak, I stand, extend my hand

to Mr. Chambers — a man I met last year at a conference. He squints, then shakes it briefly.

"Hello, Mr. Chambers. It's been twelve months, at least. I'm Declyn Bianchi. The beautiful woman beside me is my wife, Essynda." I smile at Synn, then back at him. "There must be confusion. My wife and I have been married over six months. As you can see, we're expecting our first child."

Chambers stares at Synn's belly, then at my father. "What is going on, Bianchi? Who was at the meeting a few weeks ago?" His eyes burn into me, catching the stud in my ear.

"It was my twin, Leo'ando," I say firmly, sitting back down, arm around Synn, sipping my drink.

I glance at my father. His glare could kill. I look away, catching Caroline's parents' reaction. They're furious. Leo keeps his head down.

I haven't officially met Mr. and Mrs. Dumas. Caroline herself? Spoiled, self-centered little bitch. First time I met her, she tried to pass me off as Leo. I corrected her instantly.

My appearance differs from Leo's in more ways than a casual glance could miss. Where his hair is slicked back with that polished playboy shine, mine is cropped shorter, deliberately styled to look sharp but practical. I keep a short-trimmed beard that marks me instantly apart from his clean-shaven face, and my clothing is tailored with precision — darker suits, subtle accessories, nothing like his flashy cufflinks and loud ties. Even the way I carry myself is different: Leo struts, I move with purpose.

Caroline noticed the differences at first, but not enough to stop her games. Barely an hour later, I caught her in the hallway, phone pressed to her ear, voice dripping arrogance as she bragged to whoever was on the other end about how she planned to seduce both Bianchi brothers. She laughed, tossing her hair like she'd already won, oblivious to me standing just around the corner listening. That was the moment her true nature showed — not interested in love, not even in loyalty, just in conquest and scandal.

My attention returns to the questions being directed at my brother.

"Leo'ando, why did you sign the contracts the other week?" Mr. Dumas demands. "You're engaged to my daughter."

I squeeze Synn closer. At least we've made our point. Tonight is going to be entertaining — not in a good way. Can it get any more awkward?

Chapter Twenty-Two

ESSY

"Essynda, how did you and Declyn meet?" Lillian casually asks with a smile.

I did not know to trust Lillian's words. Is she legit, or is she up to something, especially when I notice the glint in her eyes?

The server removes my empty entrée dish. "Thank you," I say with a smile to the server. He nods back to me in appreciation, then moves on to the next place setting.

Dekk leans towards me and kisses the corner of my mouth. I turn enough and return his gentle kiss to his lips. Dekk hugs me as encouragement.

I then smile at Lillian and reply, "Declyn and I met last year. He hired me as his bodyguard."

Another server places my mains in front of me. The delicious aroma sets my belly rumbling and my mouth waters. Dekk leans toward my plate and slices my steak in bite sizes for me.

"His bodyguard? You. A woman."

The attitude did not impress me. I smile and reply, "Yes. I'm fully qualified." And place the fork containing a small bite-sized piece of steak with mushroom gravy in my mouth. The instant the meat touches my tongue, it melts, and the flavors explode in my mouth. If I could get away with it, I would moan in pleasure.

"What is there to be fully qualified?" Mr. Dumas sarcastically says.

I give him one of my looks, which my old FBI partner would say would scare him because he knew I had something in mind to hurt him.

I take another bite of my food. Place my fork down and sit a little straighter and swallow my mouthful. "Mr. Dumas, even though I might only have the use of one arm, I'd probably still out-shoot you and disable you. Never underestimate a woman," I say with a smile. I pick my fork back up and take another mouthwatering bite of my meal, savoring the flavors.

The annoying man glances at Dekk. My husband smiles and nods. "You better believe it. My girl is one dangerous, kick-ass woman."

I'm halfway eating the next delicious bite. When I feel I'm being stared at. I glance up to see the newcomers looking at me as if I were an alien.

"As soon as Essynda's contract was completed, I offered her a new one for life," Dekk says with a big smile. He picks up my hand and kisses the back of it. "I fell in love with her mind, body, and soul. She has taught me so much. Essynda remained professional throughout her bodyguard contract. She is one of the best in her industry."

I lean over, kiss Dekk on his cheek, and whisper near his ear, "Thank you for saying that. I love you."

Dekk releases my hand, so I place another fork full of food into my mouth. The hair at the back of my neck rose, and the warning tingles increased. Oh, crap. Something is about to happen.

"Essy." The soft tones in my ear are the only sign my mother gives me before she starts her warning. "Get up and go to the bathroom. We need to talk."

Taking another sip of my drink, I place the glass beside my nearly empty plate, lean towards Dekk, and quietly say, "Honey, I need to go to the bathroom. One twin is bouncing on my bladder."

Conversations pause around the table, showing they are listening to our conversation. Geez, hasn't anyone heard of a pregnant woman needing the bathroom before...

"Okay, Essy. I'll help you to your feet." Dekk stands and assists me from my chair.

"Honey, why don't you walk with me?"

With a nod, Dekk offers me his arm and leads me out of the room. As we move away from our dinner group, I scan our surroundings for potential threats on the way to the nearest restroom. By making a swift hand gesture in Dekk's direction, I silently convey my desire for him to stay out of the bathroom. He acknowledges my message with a nod of understanding.

Once I step into the women's restroom, I whisper at my reflection in the mirror. "Momma, what is it?"

"Essy, thankfully, my team is nearly here." Why do I feel she is about to add a 'but,' to her words? "But the bad thing is—" And there it is. 'But.' Now I'm dreading her next sentence. "Two black vans have just pulled up out front. Six armed men have gotten out and are heading your way. Time to leave, baby girl."

Oh, hairy monkey balls. This is not good. Silently, I take a step back towards the restroom door, my heart pounding as I reach for my weapon.

With caution, I open the door slightly to see Dekk leaning against the wall with his arms crossed over his chest. I wave and signal for him to enter the restroom. He looks to his left and then to his right before stepping forward and entering the bathroom.

"Synn, what is it?" he whispers.

I whisper back, "Honey, I need you to get your cell and text Leo to move his butt to come here. We have company."

"Shit. Really?"

"Yes, really! Start texting. We're in trouble. Six armed men are heading this way."

His eyes widen, letting me know he is indeed listening, as he removes his cell from inside his jacket pocket and begins texting.

Within forty seconds, Leo is at the bathroom door.

"What is going on? Do you need a man to hold your hand to pee, Sweets?"

"Leo," I hiss through gritted teeth, trying to keep my frustration in check, "shut it." My gaze meets Dekk's, as he shakes his head in annoyance at his brother. "Hurry and get your ass inside," I demand. "Please tell me you are carrying your gun."

He walks in, glances at his brother, then at me. "Why?"

I shake my head at the fool. I glance back at Dekk. "Did you warn him about the armed men?"

"What armed men?"

"The six men with guns are heading our way."

"Why are we hiding out in the restroom?" he whines. I shake my head, take a deep breath, and count to ten.

"Because I had to get both you and Dekk to safety. That is why. Now be quiet."

Slightly opening the restroom door, I check to see what I can hear and see through the slim gap.

At first, I see nothing. Then I glimpse a stranger holding a gun, making his way towards us. I step back. "Mom, how far out are your people?" I quietly whisper.

"Mom? Who are you talking to?" Leo says a little too loudly as his voice echoes through the restroom.

Hairy monkey balls. The dickhead has done it again. He never listens.

I urge Dekk to move his brother to the stalls as I hear footsteps approach the restroom door.

Dekk pulls Leo to the side and shoves him inside a cubical. Next thing, the bathroom door bursts open. The armed stranger comes rushing in with his gun held high.

My mother's voice echoes in my ear, "Shoot. Enemy." She doesn't have to tell me twice. I'd worked it out when an armed man barged into the women's restroom. So I don't waste any time and duck to the side as the armed man lifts his gun and points it at me. We both pull the trigger at the same time.

My bullet hits the stranger's head. Blood splatters against the patterned tiles. His gunfire echoing through the tiled restroom will surely bring others here. Thankfully, his shot misses me and hits the wall instead, shattering a ceramic tile. The shooter's handgun clanks against the floor as the stranger falls into a heap.

Leo screams from the stalls, while Dekk swears a few choice words, and then calls out "Essy? Essy, are you okay?"

My mother's voice rushes into my earpiece. "Geez, Essy. You cut that one close."

"Not now, Mother! I'm a little busy," I hiss. As I turn my head, and say over my shoulder, "Dekk, I'm okay. Stay in the stalls. It's not safe to come out."

Peering through the small gap of the bathroom door, my breath catches in my throat when I spot another armed man making a beeline towards me.

Dammit. I can't catch a break.

My mother's voice echoes into my earpiece, catching me off guard. "Shoot."

Just then, the armed man spots me. As if I'm watching in slow motion, he reaches for his gun and points it in my direction. With my gum raised and my finger already on the trigger, I squeeze it multiple times, each shot muffled by the gun's silencer as my precise shots find their mark, causing the armed man to crumple onto the carpeted floor.

With no one in sight down the hallway, I retreat

from the door and shift my focus to the toilet stalls. "Boys, you better come out. We have to move. And watch out for the blood," I casually say.

Once again, I cautiously scan the hallway for any sign of movement before cautiously exiting the women's bathroom. With the dead body in the hallway, dammit, we'll have to move it out of sight before we go anywhere. I look over my shoulder at Dekk and Leo and say, "You better drag that man into the bathroom before anyone discovers him."

With the door held open, I hear Leo whining as he and his brother strain to lift the man's weight. Their footsteps scuff along the floor as they drag him into the ladies' bathroom.

"Who in the hell are these guys?" Leo demands as they dump the body next to the other one.

With a raised brow, I reply, "Seriously, Leo. You think I know?"

"Well, don't your parents know?"

I shrug my shoulders and turn towards Dekk. "Honey, we have to go. I need to get you two out of here."

With a nod of his head, Dekk reaches for my arm. "Come on. You are looking a little pale, Essy."

Yeah, well, I don't feel so good. Shooting armed men has my heart racing and my blood pressure increasing.

My mother's light tones fill my earpiece. "Essy, we have been busy checking the outside surveillance camera footage. We saw a new man exiting another vehicle parked outside. We're searching the face recognition database at the moment. Unfortunately, we do not know his identity, but he looks vaguely familiar."

Huh. What is my mother going on about? We sneak towards the staff staircase. Checking over my shoulder to make sure the coast is clear. Once we see the exit, I say, "Okay you two, I urge Leo to go through the door. "Please head to the van. My mother is waiting for us in the back parking lot. Let's go." The boys nod, and Leo begins down the back steps with Dekk not far behind him.

My father's voice interrupts me mid-step, causing me to pause. "Essy," he says. His rushed words come through my earpiece. "Four hostiles have been subdued on the upper level. Moving the bodies now."

I roll my eyes at my father's demands. Dammit. Our work is not complete. I was looking forward to sitting down. Safety comes first.

Hairy monkey balls. Coming to a stop at the top of the outer steps, I watch Dekk take two more steps before he stops and looks over his shoulder. Once our eyes meet, I say, "Boys, continue to the van without me. My father requires me back inside."

Dekk steps back up several steps, reaching for my arm. "Are you crazy? No, Essy. You are not going in alone."

"Honey, I can concentrate better if I don't have to worry about you. Please, let me do my job." I move down a step, which brings our faces together, and brush my lips over his. "I love you. Remember that." With my good arm, I wrap it around him and squeeze him hard. "Now go. My mom is waiting."

I take a step back from him, as I survey our surroundings to ensure there is no one nearby, and quietly slip back inside the building.

Just as I go through the door at the back, a waitress captures my attention just up ahead of me, balancing two plates on her arm. Something does not feel right about her.

I wait for her to disappear and quietly whisper, "Momma, did you see that woman?"

"Yes, Essy. Why?"

"Can you do a staff check?"

"Why? What is it, Essy?"

"I don't think she works here."

"What would make you say that?"

I shake my head before answering, "Does Daddy have ears to our conversation?"

"He does now. Why? What is going on?"

"Daddy, I want you to watch for a waitress carrying two plates. The only thing, she is no waitress."

My father's surprised tone fills my earpiece. "Why do you say that?"

"Well, apart from she's wearing high heels. Her work uniform does not match the other staff here. I bet she's hiding something."

"Roger that," my father replies.

I can hear my mother's voice through the earpiece, welcoming and inviting the boys into the van.

"Where is Essy?" Dekk demands.

"This is her," my mother says. "She's wearing a camera and a mic."

"Can she hear me?" I smile at my husband's concerned voice.

"Here, this is a direct earpiece to hear Essy," my mother says.

"Okay, thanks." Dekk's voice conveyed a sense of surprise.

I use my hand signal to indicate I'm okay, followed by, "Yes, Dekk. I can hear you. Now behave and allow me to do my job." I glance over my shoulder to ensure no one is coming up behind me. Then, with the hallway deserted, I slowly head upstairs toward the dining room.

As I move forward, I remain vigilant, carefully observing every nook and cranny of the floor level I am on, searching for any signs of threats. It doesn't take much time to go through the first half of the rooms along the hallway.

The harsh voices coming from the dining area made my foot stop mid-step. Oh, shit. With each step, I try to minimize any noise, inching closer to the entrance of the dining room. An unfamiliar voice suddenly breaks the silence, causing me to stop in my tracks.

I glance over my shoulder, ensuring no one is sneaking up behind me. Then, with the coast clear, I take a step forward.

"Essy." I pause. "Be careful," my mother's concerned voice fills my earpiece.

I silently count to three before quickly glancing into the dining room. My eyes zero in on the stranger standing at one end of the large dining table with a handgun pointing at my dinner associates.

What the hell!

The stranger would pass for a sibling for Dekk and Leo.

I duck back and lean against the wall as my father's voice fills my earpiece, catching me off guard. "We're in the room to your left."

With a shake of my head and a quick scan of the hallway, I take several steps and approach the other room. As I push the door open, I notice in the shadows a pair of legs on the floor.

My father's voice quietly fills my ear. "It's all clear, Essy."

Once I slip inside, I discover four men dressed similarly to the ones I shot earlier on the floor. Only these four men are on their sides. Upon closer inspection, I notice a dart sticking out from each of their necks. Well, that explains that, then. The four are still alive. I glance up and around and see two of my father's team leaning against the wall, holding bloodied medical gauze to their chest and shoulder wounds.

"Is everyone okay?" I whisper, eyeing the men on the floor again.

My father steps out of the shadows with Petersen and nods. "We moved the injured into here," my father murmurs. "As you can see, Jones and Beatty have been shot. As for those other men, they should remain unconscious for another hour or two." That is a relief.

I nod and whisper, "Okay, I'll enter the dining room and confront the stranger. First, we need to know what he wants."

I reach in my pocket for my gun, switching off the safety and sliding it back into my jacket pocket. Next, I reach into my arm sling for my second gun and slowly slide my arm out from my sling, flexing my fingers. The ache in my shoulder is dull, reminding me why I wear the arm sling.

Checking my gun, I switch the safety off and adjust the sling, placing my injured arm back in it along with my gun in its secret compartment.

"Right. Wish me luck."

My dad steps forward and places his hand on my shoulder. "Don't take any stupid risks, Essy."

I roll my eyes. "Dad, since when do I take stupid risks?" I say with a cheeky smile.

"Do you really want me to answer that with your husband listening?" Okay, he has me there.

We both nod in agreement before I turn towards the door, cautiously scanning the hallway before silently exiting the room and stealthily making my way back to the dining room entrance.

"... Are your sons going to be any longer?"

I stop when I hear the reference to Dekk and Leo.

"Leave my sons out of this. Your issues are with me, not them," Mr. Bianchi declares.

Who is the stranger?

"No, Uncle," the stranger says.

Huh? Uncle. Okay then. The stranger is Dekk and Leo's mysterious cousin.

"I will not leave them out of this. My cousins should be here to hear what you did to your brother."

What did he do? Why do I suspect Zaiden did not die from the family curse? I quickly glance through the door opening and look at the stranger — remarkable similarities to my husband. Now I have had the chance to see the man again. He could pass as Dekk's twin.

I glance over my shoulder and spot my father watching me. I use a hand signal to confirm that I am heading in.

'Essy, be careful,' he mouths.

"Look, you degenerate. You are no relation to me. Now get out of my sight," my so-called father-in-law growls.

Shit. I can see where Leo gets his intelligence from. The sound of a gun being cocked reaches my ears. Uh, oh. This will not end well.

"Jaiden, please. Calm down," I hear the shaky voice of my mother-in-law.

"You stupid woman. Do you think the son-of-a-bitch, is going to let us go? He will shoot us."

My husband's voice fills my earpiece. "No, Essy. Do not go in there."

I've had enough. I slip my fingers around the butt of my gun, keeping it out of sight. And reached down to check on my other gun, which was still in the deep pocket of my jacket. And step through the open doorway.

"Hello, everyone," I calmly say as I glance around the room to ensure everyone is keeping to their seats. "Sorry for taking so long. You know how it is when you have a baby bouncing on your bladder."

I smile and face the stranger, his startled expression revealing that he was caught off guard by my sudden appearance. "What have I missed?" I ask, scanning the room for any clues. "Has dessert arrived yet?" I glance around the table, not noticing any desserts. "The thought of sinking my teeth into a warm, homemade pie has been occupying my mind," I confess.

Well, I have. The cravings for apple and apricot pie have hounded me since I saw the treat on the menu. As I glance back at the stranger I know to tread carefully, glancing at his gun sitting in front of him. I don't know how trigger-happy this guy might be. "Oh, hello. I don't think we have met. And you are?"

I turn towards my father-in-law, then back to the stranger, and form my innocent damsel smile.

His face changes. I can tell he is wondering who I am, as I keep a smile on my face. My thoughts go to Dekk back in the van, watching. I hope Mom has begun her face recognition software on these people.

"Essy," my mother says through my earpiece. "Heads up. Two of my men have arrived. They've reached the main stairs."

With measured steps, I reach for the chair Dekk had been sitting in, drag it back away from the table, away from the stranger, and carefully sit down.

"Oh, you don't mind me sitting down, do you? My back is killing me."

I sit my butt on the chair with a sigh, and I most likely have relief covering my face. The annoying thing is getting off my feet is what I required. My hand brushes the side of my jacket, making sure the handgrip of my gun remains hidden.

With every move I make, the stranger watches me like a hawk. However, it does not take long before he no longer remains quiet and starts with his questions. "What do you think you are doing, lady? I am in charge here. I will ask the questions," he demands. "What is your name, and who are you?"

I smile again and glance around the room, taking in the unharmed, scared dinner guests, before looking back at the stranger.

"My name is Essy. I was having dinner here, and you are?" I calmly ask.

The stranger stares at the people sitting around the table before looking back at me. "I am here to discuss some personal matters," he murmurs.

I nod. "Ah." I glance towards my father-in-law before turning back to the stranger. "Are you related to Mr. Bianchi?"

The stranger nods, "Yes. Yes, I am."

"Oh, wow. I didn't know Jaiden had any other relations."

"Why would you say that?" he demands.

"Essy, our people are at the end of the front hallway," my mother whispers through my earpiece.

I casually slid my hand into my pocket.

"What did you say your name is?"

The stranger scowls and glances at my father-in-law. "Where are your sons? It is time I met them—"

I interrupt the stranger's annoying demands.

"Oh. My husband had to step out. He had a phone call to take care of."

The stranger turns my way. "Husband? Are you saying you are married into the Bianchi family?"

"Sadly, yes. How about you?"

With a raised eyebrow, he shakes his head. "No. Not married. But I am born into it."

I nod as if I am in thought. "Born... seriously! Are you Zaiden's kid?"

With a smirk, the stranger nods and glances at Jaiden. "Yes. I. Am. How did you know? Did my cousin fill you in?"

With a shrug, I reply, "No. I only recently learned that Zaiden had a girlfriend, and she gave birth after his death. Once I caught up with my husband recently, I filled him in, much to his shock. He never knew you existed."

His face changes to annoyance. "You're telling me my cousin never knew?" The stranger looks from me to my father-in-law. I shake my head at his question. He pulls a face in disgust at Jaiden. Wow, if looks could kill... Jaiden would be dead. "My mother was not his girlfriend. My mother was married to my father." He shakes his handgun around before pointing it back at my father-in-law. "From what my mother explained, you, Jaiden, killed my father."

Jaiden instantly stands, blustering and turning red. "My brother was not married."

Wow. That answered that one. My father-in-law avoided the accusation of killing his brother.

Chapter Twenty-Three

ESSY

*H*ere we go...

All that work to defuse the situation...
Gahhhh.

My husband's cousin is not happy with Jaiden standing. Not a good move when the man in question has a gun in their hand, and it appears he knows his way around a weapon.

It is time to change the subject and remove the focus from either man. I face the stranger with a loud tone and push, "So, do I send you my medical bills because I will not pay the invoice when some prick shot me."

Both Jaiden and the stranger pause and look at me.

Then the stranger frowns and says, "What do you mean someone shot you?"

I sarcastically reply, "Some asswipe shot me not that long ago. Who shoots a pregnant woman?" My brow rises, and I give the stranger a look to say, *'come on, what you say to that.'* "Was it your doing?"

A shocked look covers his face. "What? I'd never

have a pregnant woman shot. What kind of man do you think I am?"

"That is what I would like to know. It seems I was with my stupid brother-in-law when I was shot."

"Oh…" He glances down. "Sorry. I didn't know."

With an attitude building, I have had enough of stupidity, men. "You didn't know. That is not an answer. Now tell me your name."

"Essy, heads up. My men are ready to enter the dining room," my mother says in my earpiece.

No. Mom could have waited another minute or two. Instead, I lift my gun simultaneously as two of my mother's team walk through the open doorway with their weapons raised and move to either side of the room as my father rushes in after them.

Different guests around the table scream. With his gun pointed at my husband's cousins, my father shouts, "Don't move!" One of my mother's men keeps his weapon trained on the stranger, moves in, and removes the gun from his hand.

My mother's voice fills my earpiece with news no one wants to hear. "I think we have a problem."

I glance towards my father. He glances around, then at me.

"What is it?" he demands.

"There are two of them," my mother says. "He just walked into the building."

"What... two of them?" my dad questions.

My father spins and stands beside the open doorway with his gun poised.

With two of my mother's people pointing their guns at the stranger, I turn towards the open doorway.

A few seconds later, a carbon copy of my husband's cousin appears. Oh, wow. There are two of them. One wears a blue shirt, a black bomber jacket, and black dress pants. The other has a black button-up shirt under a black leather hip-length jacket with black denim jeans. Now they are both here — OMG. Both strangers would pass as Dekk and Leo.

Nearly!

"Mase, what is taking so long?" The newcomer announces as he steps into the room with a gun gripped in his hand, then freezes when he notices he's surrounded. Okay... the original stranger's name is Mase. "What the fu..." He pauses and glances at my father. Then to my mother's team members and me, then back to Mase.

"James, good of you to arrive." Mase, our first stranger, drawls through a fake smile. "You're just in time to meet Uncle!" Now we are getting somewhere. The second guy's name is James.

James turns towards Jaiden and looks him up and down. "Seriously?" Then he turns to me and glances at my pregnant belly. "So you're the baby mama. Did our cousins fill you in on the family curse?" he says with a smirk.

I shrug my shoulders. "Declyn explained everything to me. Why?"

He copied me, shrugged his shoulders, and gave me a big smile. "The boys must be very appreciative of what you have done," James boasts.

I feel as if I am going around in circles. We are not finding out why they are here with all this small talk. But at least I know their names. Well, their first names, at least.

I glance from one brother to the other. "Mase, James. Are you going to explain what you are doing here?"

The brothers smile at one another before facing me. Mase, for once, speaks, "Essy, we are here to meet my uncle and cousins. Also, to stop our mother." He looks towards the door opening. "You see. Not that long ago, my brother and I discovered we are, in fact, half-brothers and cousins."

What is he getting at...? Then it clicked. James mentioned the curse. The family ceremony comes to mind, which requires both brothers. I turn towards Jaiden, then towards Mase, then James. No... surely Jaiden and Zaiden didn't with Melissa.

The more my brain contemplated its idea, the more the weekend with Dekk and Leo came to mind. Images of the three of us together in bed...

If Jaiden and Zaiden... did the same thing... My hand moves to my belly.

"Look, brother, I think Ms. Essy worked out what is going on."

James glances around the room, then back to his brother. "Have you seen Mother?"

Jaiden stands again, sending his chair flying. "I have had enough. Matilda, grab your bag. We're leaving," Jaiden announces. He looks at me with hatred burning in his eyes. "You'll pay for this."

Before I can say a word, James retrieves a gun from behind his back and points it at Jaiden. "Not so fast, Father. Sit down and shut up."

Shocked. My body paused as my mouth hung open. Is James serious? *Father!*

Holy hairy monkey balls.

Now that confirms the elephant in the room. The only thing I do not understand is if Jaiden and Zaiden performed the ceremony saving their lives, why would Jaiden kill his brother? For what purpose? What am I missing?

I focus on Jaiden just as he steps away from the table. He reaches into his suit jacket as Mase pulls another gun from under his jacket and points it at Jaiden. "Not so fast, Uncle. Now take a seat. We have matters to discuss."

Without realizing it, I blurt out, "Mom, are you watching this?"

"Yes, Essy," Mom murmurs in my earpiece. "By the stunned look on Declyn and Leo face's they cannot believe the turn of events either."

You can say that again. Talk about an understatement.

Movement near my right has me turning my head...

"You lying, cheating bastard," my mother-in-law Matilda screeches.

With everyone's attention on the brothers and my mother-in-law, no one is watching the doorway. Instead, the non-waitress appears with a gun in her hand, pointing straight at Jaiden. The look in her eyes is scary as the white orbs bulge, and her lips part. "You low life," she announces. "Finally." Her smile becomes feral. "After all these years — revenge for my beloved." The sound of gunfire echoes through the dining room. "Eat lead," she shrieks. Before I can move and slide off the chair, sharp, hot pain hits me, sending me back against the chair.

Women's screams fill the room, and all hell breaks loose — more gunfire sounds, with loud thumps, grunts, and groans.

I notice two things. One — my father-in-law, with a satisfied look on his face, a gun in his hand pointing towards me. Oh, hair, monkey balls. That can't be good. Two — I look down as blood rivets down my front.

Oh, shit. "Help," I gurgle as a wet bubble pops between my lips.

My breath catches as the room spins. My mother screams through the earpiece as Mase fills my vision.

"Essy... Shit. You've been shot," he states, simultaneously thrusting something white against my chest. Shit, that hurts. "Stay with me, Essy." His voice fades a little. "James, get your ass here. Essy's been shot. Let the others deal with Mother."

"We have to get her out of here," I vaguely hear a male voice say just before everything turns black.

Chapter Twenty-Four

DEKK

I must be in a nightmare. While my wife ensured my brother and I were safe, she returned to a dangerous situation.

The vision on the monitors in the van displays a live video feed from Synn, her father, and his men. I was shocked to discover Synn had been wearing a tiny video camera.

I just witnessed the expression on my mother's face when she found out that her husband had fathered a child with someone else.

My wife's words barely register in my ear, "Mom, are you watching this?"

"Yes, Essy. By the look on Declyn and Leo face's they cannot believe the turn of events," my mother-in-law replies.

I'm overwhelmed with disbelief at my father's lies and the revealed truth, as my mind struggles to process the fact that Leo and I have a half-brother. Holy moly. I direct my gaze towards Leo to catch his reaction. We have a half-brother.

Right as I was about to ask for his thoughts, our mother's voice shrieks through the speaker. "You lying, cheating bastard." My attention shifts back to the wall of screens, where I catch a glimpse of my mother's angry face. As I scan the various monitors, my heart plummets when I catch sight of my father on the top right screen, his grip tight around a gun.

Out of nowhere, the angry screams of a woman echoed through the air, accompanied by the deafening bursts of gunfire, throwing everything into disarray. My mother-in-law raises her voice, her frustration clear as she desperately tries to engage with Synn. Only for my wife's words not to fill my earpiece.

Oh, no, what happened?

It feels as if I am watching a fiction film on the monitors, where nothing seems to make sense. My father's gun is pointing in Synn's direction. His satisfied grin morphs into a look of shock, as his eyes widen when he glances down at his chest. A dark patch spreads and his face contorts with disbelief. He glances at my mother, his eyes pleading for help, before collapsing to the floor.

On a different monitor, Synn's father's people forcefully detain a waitress who is armed with a gun. Through my earpiece, I hear one of the brother's voices calling out Synn's name, their tone filled with desperation. "Essy... Shit. You've been shot," Mase says as his face fills the screen of Synn's monitor before he thrusts a white tablecloth napkin at Synn. "Stay with me, Essy," Mase yells, his voice filled with urgency. "James, get your ass here. Essy's been shot. Let the others deal with Mother."

'No. No, no, no, Synn.' I don't know if I screamed her name in my head or out loud. Panic overwhelms me as I watch the unimaginable on the screens. My wife can't be shot. Just the thought fills me with such terror that my heart pounds against my ribs as if it might give out at any moment. Tuning out my brother's worried words, I bolt from the van and sprint towards the restaurant entrance, desperate to be with my wife.

My foot lands on the first step at the front entry. It takes a few precious seconds to realize other people are rushing toward me, one of them carrying a woman in his arms — my wife.

My feet refuse to budge from the step, taking in the sight of my wife's lifeless body. "Essy!" I call out, my voice echoing around me as if I'm in a bubble. Reality returns when the piercing sound of emergency sirens reaches my ears. My lungs fill, and I sigh with gratitude, realizing someone has contacted the paramedics, ensuring help is on the way.

Thankful for my legs keeping me upright, my feet move, and my anxiety grows as I approach my unconscious wife, her limp body held gently by the stranger I believe is Mase. Our resemblance is so uncanny that it's like looking at Leo and me. It's no wonder I can easily tell that he is my relative. My father's actions have left a trail of unanswered questions.

"How is she?" I demand as I approach with my arms

raised, ready to take my wife. My heart races with worry.

Regret and sadness fill his gaze as he meets my eyes. He shakes his head and glances down at Synn. "She's losing blood."

Even without the Mase saying anything, it was clear from the dark, bloodstained cloth over Synn's chest that she's bleeding. My gaze sweeps across her entire form, and without hesitation, I reach out and touch my wife's belly. "Do you know if she is shot anywhere else?" Concern laced each word. As move one hand on her upper belly. Within seconds, I feel one babe kick and shift around. Then I move my other hand to her lower abdomen and feel more movement. Relief fills me.

"As far as I can tell, she was only shot in the upper chest," Mase explains as flashing lights and a loud siren approach. "My brother and I were trying to prevent anyone from getting hurt. We failed. I'm sorry."

I turn in time to see an ambulance arrive, quickly followed by several police cars with their lights flashing and sirens blaring as the ambulance stops beside the curb.

Synn's mother runs straight to her daughter, flashing her FBI badge simultaneously, reaching for Synn's limp hand. I turn and glance over my shoulder for my brother. Where did he go? The two medics issued orders for Synn to be placed on the stretcher. A second ambulance arrives, pulling up behind the first.

"What do we have?" one medic demands as he lifts the cloth onto her chest. Blood seeps from a jagged dark hole. Oh, gods, that looks bad.

I'm too busy watching my wife on the gurney to think straight. Then I remembered the medic had asked a question. "My wife. Essy is seven months pregnant and has been shot." It does not take the two men long to load Synn into the back of the ambulance, removing her arm sling containing her gun and passing it to Synn's mother.

"Sir, where is the shooter?" one medic asks as he redresses Synn's wound. The other medic inserts a cannula into her arm and attaches a bag of liquid to the long tubing. A blood pressure cuff is placed on her other arm, and they begin the process of her vitals.

I mumble, "Inside. Captured," as I watch the medics begin their medical assessment of Synn's vitals.

"Blood pressure 85 over 57. Oxygen levels are lower than I like. We need to get moving," the medic says. He makes eye contact with me and asks, "Who will accompany us?"

Both Synn's mother and I respond with, "Me."

We look at one another, then at the medic. "I'm her mother," Synn's mom clarifies. He eyes us both and shakes his head.

"Right... How about, Mom, you go up the front, and Husband, you stay back with us." I nod and meet Synn's mom's stare. She gives me a nod and hurries to the front of the vehicle.

We need to get to the hospital on time. Without my courageous wife and babies, I don't know what I'd do.

I feel a hand on my shoulder and look back to see who it is. "I am so sorry. My brother and I had hoped to prevent our mother from hurting anyone. She has been hell-bent on getting revenge. I'm sorry," James pleads.

He turns and moves away from the ambulance. I glance up to see a woman wearing waitress clothing being escorted out of the building by two men with her hands behind her back.

I spot Leo and call out to him, "Leo, stay with Mom. Make sure she gets home." He nods and walks up the steps, and disappears inside.

Another ambulance arrived as two other medics wheeled another ambulance gurney out of the building containing my father, followed by my mother, in my brother's arms.

I climb into the back of the ambulance and sit down beside Synn. The door at the back of the vehicle closes, and within seconds the engine starts, and we are away.

The medic in the back with us keeps monitoring Synn's condition. "We are going to need plasma. The patient is losing far too much blood." He glances up at Synn's mother. "Are you a blood match for your daughter?"

As Synn is adopted, I am about to say no, but instead, my mother-in-law states, "Yes. We are a match!" Say what? How can that be possible?

The next thing I hear is the driver cursing at the sound of crackling voices from a CB radio.

"Franky, we have a problem. There's been a pile-up before the bridge. We can't get through. All the other roads are banking up."

I now know the medic's name as Franky curses under his breath and rechecks Synn, then looks toward the driver. "Barry, turn off. We'll have to call in SkyHealth."

"Yes, I agree. I just received word that the hospitals on Staten Island are all on bypass. They have been filled with emergencies. Placing an order for medevac now."

"What's going on?" my mother-in-law demands.

Franky answers, "We have to organize a chopper to take your daughter to a bigger hospital that can care for her."

"Is that possible? Can you arrange for a SkyHealth medevac in time?"

"I hope so, but your daughter requires blood now. Move down here. I will have to start a line between you both. It is the only thing I can do while we wait."

I glance down at my pale wife's face. Please, Synn. You have to make it.

Chapter Twenty-Five

ESSY

The slow beeping guides my mind through the thick fog. The heavyweight against my hand tightens, and I wonder what has my hand in its grip. My surroundings are cloaked in darkness until the sound of a familiar voice breaks through.

A male voice.

"When are you going to tell her? She deserves to know the truth."

"Now is not that time, Declyn. When Essynda is recovered, home and safe, I will sit down with her and Laini."

Hang on a minute… That is my mother's voice. What is she talking about? What is my husband confronting her with?

Come on, guys. Keep talking. Let me know what is going on. What is my mother going to tell me?

Before I can hear another sentence, my mind is submerged in darkness's thick fog.

"*B*aby, come on. It is time to wake up."

Huh? What?

"Come on, Synn. We need to see your beautiful eyes."

Dekk? What is Declyn going on about now? I am so tired. Let me sleep.

"Essy. Bloody wake-up. You have been asleep long enough." Huh? What? Laini? What in the world is Laini doing in my bedroom? Come on. Does anyone remember boundaries? Privacy... even?

"Sweets, come on, darlin'. My brother needs to eat and shower. He can only do that if you wake up."

What the hell? Is Leo in my room? Who in the hell is allowing everyone into my bedroom?

"Time to wake up, pumpkin."

Daddy? Why is my father here?

"Essynda, it is time to wake up, baby girl."

Huh... Mom?

I just want to sleep, Mom. Please allow me to sleep.

Darkness increases around me, and I hear no more.

Chapter Twenty-Six

ESSY

*W*hat the...?

Why can't I roll over?

I try to move in my bed, only to discover a heavy warm body at my back. I tap on the heavy arm I can feel draped over my chest and under my breasts.

"Dekk. Move over. I need to move," I croak. Huh? What is wrong with my voice? I push my ass back into Dekk. I have to move. My throat is dry. I need a drink. "Dekk. Come on. Move," I demand as I nudge my butt into his pelvis.

I feel his arm tighten against me.

"Essy?" I hear Dekk moan. "Baby... Thank god. You're waking up."

What the hell?

I move my butt again. I seriously need a drink and to empty my bladder.

"Dekk. I need the bathroom," I groan. "Can you get me a drink?"

"Baby. You're awake. Hang on. I gotta call for the nurse."

What? What nurse? Why would I need a nurse?

Dekk releases me and moves his body. I go to roll onto my back, and I stop in my tracks.

"Argh." Pain. Where in the hell did this pain come from? Burning pain radiates from my chest and shoulder. Have I injured myself?

"Essy, try not to move too much. You have to be careful of your injuries," Dekk says. A sharp beep sounds a couple of times near my head.

"What... injuries?" I croak.

"Babe, you had been shot — again."

"What?" Shot... again... how?

After a few more seconds of battling fatigue, I lift my eyelids and just about blind myself from the overhead light.

The sound of a door hinge grabs my attention. I blink twice, and the next thing I realize is a strange woman standing over me.

A dark-haired woman glances above me with a smiling face and reaches for something. "My name is Maybeth, and I am your nurse today. How are you feeling, Mrs. Bianchi?" she asks in a friendly voice. "It is good to see you are awake."

What is going on? Why do I have all this pain?

"She's in pain, nurse. Plus, she wants a drink," Dekk explains to the strange woman.

Who in the hell is she? Where am I?

I blink a few more times and finally focus on my surroundings.

Oh, hairy monkey balls. I am in the hospital.

I search for Dekk. I need to see his face.

"Dekk…"

"I'm here, Essy." I feel my hand being squeezed, and I glance to my right. My sexy husband fills my vision. I notice how scruffy he appears, with dark circles under his eyes and pale. Bloody hell. How long have I been here?

My mouth opens and closes several times before croaking, "How long?"

"Babe, you have been unconscious for two weeks. I have not left your side."

"How?" I blink several times and glance at the nurse.

"How did you end up here again?" I nod, feeling my heartbeat increase, and he sighs. "Essy, you were shot."

Shot… he has said that already. How?

Pressure on my arm changes my focus. Then, I realize the blood pressure cuff is functioning and becoming tighter. Then, I watch the digital screen, and my blood pressure results appear.

"101 over 71," the woman says. "A little low, but you are improving."

Improving… Seriously?

While watching the nurse, I don't know what happened, but the urge to go to the loo stopped. What the…?

The nurse's click-clacking against the keyboard brings my attention to the tall mobile stand with a big monitor about an inch taller than her. I watched her enter the data on the screen computerized medical chart. In front of her is a two-draw cabinet under the pullout keyboard, which I remember from my last stay in the hospital, housing my medications. How times have changed in a hospital, from the clipboards with paper forms to electronic medical trolleys.

She turns enough, leans down to the side of the bed, and grabs something. What is she holding? She glances up and notices me watching. "It is time to change your bag, Mrs. Bianchi." Bag? What bag? "You have a catheter inserted, which means no getting up from your bed. Not until we remove it."

"Huh?"

Chapter Twenty-Seven

DEKK

*T*hey should make hospital beds more comfortable!

Propped up against Synn's pillows, I try to shuffle a little to adjust the kink in my back without disturbing my wife.

With Synn in my arms, knowing she only sleeps has my anxiety down and not near death's door. Thank goodness Synn is finally conscious. She has had me worried. I refused to leave the hospital in case anything happened.

The doctor checked her and the twins an hour and a half ago. Finally, the catheter was removed, allowing Synn to get out of bed. I wheeled her into her bathroom and the shower. With my help and being mindful of her dressings, Synn enjoyed a hot shower while I washed her hair.

Once I had Synn washed, rinsed, dried, and dressed, Synn was adamant that she could brush her teeth while I was using the shower. Finally showered and feeling human again, I dressed in the clean clothes Leo had brought me.

After two weeks, I finally got to kiss my wife. I watched Synn eat the food the nursing staff had brought her. Before she quietly fell back to sleep.

So here I am, leaning back against her pillows with my chin resting against her head, watching over my sleeping, beautiful wife. At least now she is aware I am holding her. The nagging feeling grows, reminding me it is time to phone Synn's parents and inform them Synn has woken.

Since Synn has been unconscious, my mother has treated me like shit and pressured me to be by her side instead of my wife's. So yes. My family has been through hell, but so have I and my pregnant, injured wife.

My father died from a gunshot wound to the chest. Mase and James's mother finally got her revenge for her dead husband, my uncle. It was a pity Aunt Melissa had not pulled her trigger thirty seconds earlier. She could have prevented my father from shooting Synn. He was determined to end my relationship with my wife and nearly succeeded. The annoying fact is Melissa escaped from the police. Another reason I have not left my wife's side is because I'm her husband and will protect what is mine.

Several days after Synn was admitted to the hospital, her parents discovered the paper trail to confirm my uncle's wedding and the birth of twins Mase and James.

After a couple of weeks of surprises and home truths, Synn's parents reveal a massive secret. A secret so big I don't know if my wife and her sister will handle the news. Life can be cruel, mysterious, and strange all at the same time.

I stretch out my hand and take hold of my cell phone from the side table. While Synn was awake, I always had it on silent mode and face-down.

As soon as the screen lights up, there are seventeen notifications waiting. There are multiple missed calls on my phone, including three from Synn's parents, two from Laini, four from my mother, two from Mace and James, and one from my brother. My brother deliberately sent me five text messages, anticipating that I would reply to them before returning his phone call.

Without listening to any messages or reading Leo's texts, I tap the screen for Synn's parent's phone number.

Within two rings, I hear Synn's mother's voice. "Declyn, has there been any change?"

Keeping my voice low, I calmly reply, "Hello, Suzanna. I have good news—"

Before I say another word, my mother-in-law asks, "Is Essynda okay?" I shift my cell away from my ear and her high-pitched tones. "What has happened?"

"Suzanna, let me answer," I demand. "Essy woke."

"Thank goodness." Relief filled Suzanna's voice. "How is she?"

I glance down at Synn, noticing she is still sleeping. "Essy woke about an hour and a half ago. The doctor came in and saw her. She has since had a shower, had something to eat, and is now sleeping," I say, pressing my lips to the top of Synn's warm head.

"Thank you for letting us know."

"Susanna, I said I would keep you updated. Now, has Melissa been captured?"

Suzanna paused before answering, "Umm. No. She has gone underground." Damn it. That is not what I wanted to hear. "Sorry, Declyn. Our people are still searching for her, along with the police."

I do not trust Melissa. Chances are, she will still come after Leo and me. "Thanks, Suzanna. I want my wife safe."

"I completely agree, Declyn. We will be over at the hospital in an hour."

"Okay, Suzanna. Can you notify Laini, please? We'll see you then." To avoid any further conversation, I end the call before my mother-in-law can utter another word, ensuring my phone is on silent and placing it on the side table.

Chapter Twenty-Eight

ESSY

The enticing scent of Declyn was the first thing that greets me from my sleep, then to notice his muscular arms wrapped around me even better until the odor I detest encourages my mind to clear enough from the sleeping fog to recognize I'm back in the hospital. Why is my husband in bed with me if I'm in the hospital?

Movement across my belly alerts me that one twin is awake and moving about. My mouth and throat are parched, pushing my tongue against my teeth. I require a drink — now. I wonder if I have a jug of hospital water or if my parents have smuggled a juice bottle for me.

Slowly, I force my eyes open. Once I can focus, I see my mom sitting there reading a book while my dad is leaning against the wall with his eyes closed. After several seconds, my coordination kicks in, and I finally tap Dekk's arm with my hand. I hope someone has juice here for me. I really require a drink.

"Synn?" Dekk mumbles beside my ear. "You waking up, babe?"

Even with a foggy brain, I realize that was not the first time Dekk had called my Synn.

What is it with the twins and their nicknames for me?

I nod and croak out, "Drink. I need a drink."

My mother looks up from her book. She smiles at me, stands, and walks to the side. Within moments, she is back at my side with a glass of juice and a straw. Oh, thank goodness. I form a small smile and manage, "Thanks, Mom," as Mom places the straw near my mouth.

I wrap my lips around the thin white and blue paper-striped tube and suck. The refreshing coolness of sweet nectar fills my mouth and goes straight down my parched throat. After several mouthfuls, I release the straw, taking a breath before glancing back at Mom and nodding. "Thanks for that, Mom. It's just what I needed."

She smiles and then frowns. "How are you feeling, baby girl?" she says as she places the glass back on the little table. "We have been worried."

"I've been worried myself. How did I get reshot?" I notice Mom glance towards Dekk and then back at me. Okay... what are they not saying?

"Baby girl, what is the last thing you remember?"

Why do people ask me that question?

I scrunch my face in thought, an old habit I had as a kid. It was one way to make my mom smile when she was sad. Nothing comes to mind. I know whatever my memories are... hiding — remaining in the back of my mind a little longer. I must have been hurt badly, or my mind would not be playing tricks on me. I shake my head, glance back up, and meet Mom's worried eyes.

Dekk's arms give me another squeeze before I feel his lips press against the top of my head.

"Little one, don't go worrying," my father says. "Your body has been in shock and is recovering."

I glance up as he steps away from the wall and approaches the bed. Our eyes meet, and we smile. "I know, Dad. It did not take me long to figure it out. My shoulder is killing me. I feel like crap, and the hospital smells as it usually does." My memories are just out of reach on the edge of my mind. I turn my head enough and meet Mom's eyes and smile. Why do I have the feeling my parents are about to say something...huge. "Okay, Mom, Dad. What is it? There is something on your mind. Come on, spill."

Mom turns and glances at Dad. I can see they are worried about something. But what? They nod at one another, move towards the bed with their chairs, and sit down.

I nod my head at the two of them and smile. Seconds tick by, and I feel awkward. The quicker they say whatever it is, the faster we can move on. I wonder if my sister should be here for this conversation.

Dekk kisses the top of my head again and makes himself comfortable. Great... it seems Dekk already knows what my parents are about to say.

Mom takes in a deep breath. I can see she is worried

about whatever is on her mind. She smiles, glances towards Dad, then Dekk, and back at me.

"Baby girl... You know how your father and I love you..." Oh, great, now I am worried. What is wrong? Is my mom sick or something?

Dad murmurs something under his breath beside Mom, which I miss. She gulps and nervously smiles at me.

"Essynda, what I am about to say will be shocking, but please listen to me." Now I am worried. I glance at Dad, then back to Mom. "You might remember me telling you how I met your father on my first FBI undercover case."

Why is Mother discussing something so long ago? I nod to her words to encourage her to continue and watch Dad fidget from the corner of my eye.

"You see. Jason was my work partner on that case." Yes, I know they had met while working for the FBI. That is no secret. "The case involved several fertility clinics." She gulps, takes another breath, and continues. "Because I was not married or involved with anyone, I had agreed to be on the assignment, which involved me working undercover as a wife who was having difficulty becoming pregnant." Huh. Is Mom trying to say... I stop my thoughts. "You see," she gulps, glances at Dad, he nods to her, and then she nods back to him, "I went through all the invasive procedures. During these tests, the specialists discovered my fallopian tubes and that part of my uterus was badly scarred, most likely from a previous infection." Oh, shit. No woman ever wants to hear that. "I was started on a round of medication to harvest my eggs."

I glance at Dad, then back to Mom, and nod.

"You see, Essy. Your father also went through all the different tests, medication, and procedures." I nod again. I am not sure if whatever Mom is about to say will be bad or good. "While undercover, I had five viable embryos placed in storage, as you would when going through the procedures. I had the sixth implanted, which had taken."

What... my mother had been pregnant?

She has always said how she could not fall pregnant.

"At the time, the facility was more about collecting money than helping couples conceive and carrying a child to term. These clinics would also sell viable embryos and inform their patients their embryos had become unviable and died." Oh, my. How tragic. They were going through all those procedures and later being told that their precious embryos had not survived when they had been sold in reality. So were the clinics stopped?

Hang on... I'm missing something here. Mom mentioned she had her viable embryos placed in deep freeze, and this facility was into selling embryos. Again, I glance back at her face.

"By the time the case was complete, people were sent to jail, and the clinics shut down. It was discovered that not just mine, but also that five other couples' embryos had gone missing. Thankfully, we located the other couple's embryos. As for mine, all but two had been located." Why do I have a funny feeling about this story? Mom glances back towards Dad. He nods his head for her to continue. "Anyway, I was still pregnant with Jason's child." I glance at Dad and watch as he squeezes Mom's hand with a solemn face. "I was seven months pregnant when I went into early labor. There was no explanation for why it happened. I started to bleed, and we lost our baby boy. I was devastated, and so was Jason." Oh my god. A baby boy. No. How tragic for my parents. "From something so tragic, it brought us together."

Mom smiles at Dad, and they hug one another. Something sliding down my cheek caught my attention. It hadn't occurred to me I had been crying.

My poor parents, all their anguish and pain. They had lost so much. The original baby, then the other embryos. What they must have gone through.

"After losing the baby, there were complications. We were informed I could never carry another child again."

Oh, my poor mother. What she has gone through. I wipe my face and wait for her to continue. But there is a lot more to her story. I have the feeling something big also occurred.

"When Jason and I saw you that day in front of the orphanage, we knew we would adopt you." I smile. I was relieved the day I met them. They changed my life for the better. "What I am about to say will be hard to hear. Jason and I were shocked but ecstatic and proud at the same time. We should have said something back then... but we wanted to let you know when the time was right." What in the world... Tell me what? "You see, Essy. Last year, you, Laini, Jason, and I went through some medical testing for work." I remember the tests. I had to rearrange two of my meetings to attend. Laini was not impressed, but gave in and arrived just in time for our appointment to make our foster parents happy.

"We were curious and eager to test out the new DNA testing kits. We wanted to surprise you with information regarding your biological parents." Huh? DNA testing. My birth parents. "Well, the surprise was on us."

I glance at Mom and Dad, smiling at me with a big, gleeful grin. What is going on? What am I missing?

"Essy. We discovered not just yours, but also Laini's biological parents." Say what? Surprised is an understatement for how I feel right now, after all these years.

I allow her words to sink in. Annoyance grows and simmers to anger with the reality of her words. So they discovered my parents and have not told me! And Laini's dead parents are not her biological parents? What in the hell is going on?

"What are you trying to tell me, Susanna?" Forget me calling her — Mom. She has kept vital information from me. "Tell me what you know." I have had enough. I want answers now.

My mother's smile fades when I growl her name. She realizes I am not happy. "Baby girl, we discovered where our other embryos had gone." Her face is wet with fresh tears and smiles. "Both you and Laini are our biological children." Huh? "I am trying to say that Jason and I are your biological parents. After you were shot, I could give you my blood in a life-saving transfusion to save your life."

Chapter Twenty-Nine

ESSY

W hat the heck?

My adoptive parents are really my biological parents!

Both Lain and I are their long-lost, missing children. I should say long-lost missing embryos.

Oh, my god. Laini is my real biological sister.

We had always wished we could be actual sisters. Well, it looks like wishes come true.

Holy heck.

What a way for my parents to spring this on me!

Am I shocked? Damn right I am.

Am I feeling speechless, mystified — that would also be a yes.

When I become aware of my mouth wide open, I close my it slowly and turn my head sideways to catch a glimpse of my husband's face. As his eyes meet mine, I can see the lack of surprise in his gaze. His arms tighten around me, providing a comforting embrace that reassures me of he's here for me.

"Baby girl, please say something," my father urges. I turn and face my worried father with guilt written all over his face. Well, he should be guilty and anxious. They both could have said something way before now.

Oh, my god. My sister...

"Does Laini know?"

My parents shake their heads. No.

Okay. At least I am not the only one kept in the dark.

I watch my mother lift her oversized handbag, removing an object wrapped in fabric. It does not take me long to realize it is my gun. She gets up from her chair and opens my little set of drawers, placing the object inside.

My eyebrow raises as I watch her sit back down. She notices the look on my face. "I know you would feel safer knowing you have your gun with you." She's not wrong there. "Plus, I feel better knowing you have your gun close by with Melissa on the loose."

What is she talking about? Melissa is on the loose... A vague memory — a screaming woman. The sound of gunfire.

Oh, hairy monkey balls. You have to be kidding me. I think I remember how I was shot.

My bloody father-in-law. He is the one who shot me.

Chapter Thirty

DEKK

The minute Synn remembers, I can sense it in my gut. At first, she was frozen in disbelief, but then her whole body started shaking, fueled by anger rather than fear.

Bloody Suzanna. If she had delayed mentioning Melissa to Synn a bit longer, my wife could have been resting without staying on alert.

Thankfully, her parents knew to keep their mouths shut and not mention anything about my dad.

I hope my marriage to Synn continues, as selfish as I am. Once she knows who shot her, everything will change. Bloody hell. What a mess.

Thankfully, my wife fell asleep with her head resting on my chest and my arms around her body. My heart fills with uncertainty, knowing she grips her handgun under her bedsheet. Synn was adamant about wrapping her fingers around the weapon while she slept. Talk about keeping me on my toes.

The only warning that someone is about to

enter is a gentle tap on the door. With a slow, deliberate motion, the door swings open, revealing a nurse. A woman, vaguely familiar, stood in a pair of nurses' scrubs. Her non-medical shoes are the only warning she is not a nurse or staff member of the hospital.

I think we're in trouble!

With my hand still under the sheet, I gently tap against Synn's leg to grab her attention.

"Hello," I say to the woman. "Are you here for Essy's tray?"

The stranger glances towards the empty food tray, to Synn, then back to me.

She shakes her head. "No. I'm here for you." Why does her voice sound like I have heard it somewhere before?

Then it clicks — the pier and the restaurant. The strange woman is my aunt. Uh-oh.

Plucking courage out of thin air and hoping my voice sounds normal, I say, "I would guess you might be my long-lost aunt?"

She smirks. "I would say you are my insufferable nephew." At least her words answered my question. Oh, no. I definitely have to tread carefully — this woman wants the males in my family dead.

"You shot my father. Why?"

I hope Synn wakes from my tapping against her leg under the sheet.

Melissa's eyes flick to Synn, then back to me with her eyebrow raised. "Really? Are you serious right now?"

"I was not in the restaurant when you showed up. Explain to me why you shot my father," I demand.

"For my love — my husband," she sarcastically whines. "I'll waste time and explain it to you."

I nod and encourage her to sit in the chair. At least then, she will not be hovering. Someone in the family better come along and visit. For once, I would prefer Synn's parents to drop by.

She sits, glances towards the door, then around the room, and focuses on me for a second before staring at Synn. "Do you love her?"

I don't hesitate. "Yes."

"Does she know about the family curse?"

I press my lips to the top of Synn's head. I nod and reply, "As much as I do."

She nods and glances down at the floor. "Who explained the family curse to you... was it your grandfather or pathetic father?"

With a shrug of my shoulders, I reply, "My father. Why?" Hang on, why would she mention my dead grandfather?

Her eyes meet mine in a scorching blaze.

"Your father is nothing but a two-timing lying piece of shit. Who doesn't give a rat's ass to anyone but himself!" she states matter-of-factly. Well, I know my father only cared about himself. Her words are nothing new to me. It always came down to money with my father.

"You're not telling me anything new. What is it you're trying to say?"

I notice her eyebrow raise at my words. At least she

knows how I feel. I am not a fan of my father — dead or alive.

"Well, now. How well do you know your grandfather?"

I shrug my shoulders. "Not well. My father had a falling out with the man. My grandfather is dead — "

Her eyes widen, and she shakes her head. "What? Your grandfather is not dead. Why would you say such a thing?"

Huh? "My father informed Leo and me that our grandfather had died in a tragic accident twenty-five years ago. Unfortunately, his body could not be recovered."

Melissa's face changes, and she sneers at me. "Your grandfather is very much alive. You stupid boy. Your father lied to you."

What the hell?

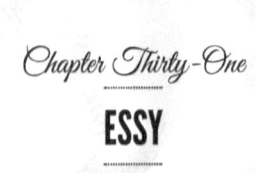

Chapter Thirty-One

ESSY

*D*ekk did not have to wake me to give me the heads up we have a visitor. I sensed her before she enters. Poor Dekk. Finding out your grandfather is still alive and that your father has lied to you all your life... He must be distraught.

"Look, lady," he manages in a calm voice. "If my grandfather is alive... why hasn't he reached out to Leo and me?" Good question. Why hasn't the grandfather contacted Declyn?

"That is something you will have to speak with your grandfather about," she casually says.

Listening to the tone in her voice, she's here to harm my husband and me. If she has her way, we will not be leaving here alive. Thank goodness I have my gun gripped in my hand.

"What are you saying? There's something else to do with the family's so-called curse?"

"You could say that."

"Look, lady, stop going around in circles and tell me." Yep. My man is agitated. That is not a good sign.

"Declyn, is your wife having twins?"

I feel him flinch. "Yes. What has that got to do with anything?"

"You silly little man. It has everything to do with it."

"Why?" I agree. Why?

"The curse began by a witch back in Salam. October 1692."

"What? The Salem witch trials. You have to be kidding me."

"It had. I researched this so-called family curse as much as I could. I want to protect my sons."

"So, what did you discover?" Yes, what did she discover?

"In 1680, twin boys arrived with their family to live near the township of Salem Town. Their names were Ericson and Benjamin Bianchi."

"What... you're saying my ancestors were already living in America in the sixteen hundreds?"

"They lived in America for over five generations before moving back to Italy."

"So what happened for this curse to be placed on the Bianchi family?"

"You see, Benjamin had fallen in love with a local lass from the Salem Village named Elizabeth. Her family was a rich aristocrat family well known."

"And what does an aristocrat family have to do with my family curse?"

"If you keep quiet, I'll explain," she whines.

I nudge Dekk against his thigh to inform him I am

awake, and he should calm down. There is no telling what the woman might do.

"All right. As you were telling..." Dekk casually says understanding message.

I hear the woman huff before continuing her tale. "It was a secret through town. Elizabeth's aunt was a healer."

"A healer? What, like a doctor or witch?" Dekk murmurs.

"A bit of both. Now shh," Melissa complains. "Now Benjamin had to travel overnight and stay in the Rowley Village to drop off some supplies for his uncle, who owned a trade store. His brother Ericson was to inform Elizabeth that Benjamin could not take her to the dance that night. Instead of Ericson explaining his brother's wishes to Elizabeth, he dressed in his brother's evening clothes and pretended to be Benjamin."

Uh-oh. Why do I feel Ericson is like Leo? Why do I have a bad feeling regarding Ericson?

"What did Ericson do to Elizabeth?" Dekk asked. Yes — what Dekk said.

"I like that. Straight to the point," she sneers. "Long story short, Ericson pretended to be his brother. Seduced his brother's fiancée and raped her, leaving her broken and battered."

"What? No. Did he kill her?"

"No. But Elizabeth had thought it was Benjamin until she had seen a scar on Ericson's chest."

"A scar?"

"Yes, a scar. Something Ericson received when he dueled six months before over a married woman."

"Sounds like a selfish troublemaker." Reminding me of Leo and some of his pathetic moves over the years. "What happened to Elizabeth?"

"With her injuries tended to by her aunt, Elizabeth slowly regained her strength, but the emotional wounds ran deep, causing her to push Benjamin away, despite her love for him. Benjamin's presence always served as a painful reminder to Elizabeth of what Ericson had done."

"That is understandable. Elizabeth had been beaten and violated. But I want to know what happened regarding the family curse."

"Once it was established it had been Ericson and not Benjamin who attacked Elizabeth. Her family gathered and performed a specific ritual."

"A ritual... seriously?"

"Yes. Seriously. It was determined for the Bianchi line to continue. Twins would be born, belonging to two brothers."

"What do you mean, belonging to two brothers?"

"Exactly what I said. Three people are required to perform the ceremony: twin brothers and one female. Once the female is impregnated, both adult twins survive. However, if only one twin brother impregnates the female, the other twin brother will die."

I hear Dekk mumble near my ear, "Huh? I was led to believe the twins only had to perform the ceremony, and that was it... No pregnancy. No babies involved." I need to inform my husband of the information I have discovered. All this curse stuff is bogus. Dekk's voice brings my focus back. "So you're saying my wife is pregnant with both mine and my brother's child? That is why we both survived."

"Yes. The same with my sons. One of them is married and had twins last year."

"So are you saying... if the men — twins of my family do not work together and perform the ceremony, both impregnating the woman, one of the adult twins will die?"

Oh, boy. This woman is milking the family curse stuff for all its worth.

"Basically, yes. Both men have to treat the female with respect for the ceremony to work and twins to be born," she sneers.

You have to be kidding me. The male line of the Bianchi family are well known for producing twins.

"Why are you here? My father is dead." What...? My thoughts were interrupted by Dekk's words. Dead. When? "Thanks to his secrets. My brother and I never knew about you, your sons, or what happened to my uncle or grandfather."

"I am here to make sure your father's line is finished. After that, my sons will take over the Bianchi family business. Where they should have been from the start."

I feel Dekk still.

If Dekk didn't know before, he knows now.

We are in trouble.

"Look, Melissa. My brother and I knew nothing about you or our cousins. If you had contacted us initially, things would have been different."

"What do you mean would have been different?"

"For one, we would have made sure our father was stopped. Second, Leo and I have had enough of his bullshit interfering in our lives."

"What have you had to worry about? You have had everything handed to you."

"Look, lady. Never presume you know everything. Because you don't."

"Says the boy who has had everything given to him."

"Seriously! My father arranged for Leo and me to be married to people we either did not know or liked. Did you know he was in the process of ending my marriage to Essy and having it annulled? Or the final straw was when he tried to kill her and my children."

He what? So he is the one who shot me.

Jaiden shot me at the restaurant. I remember now.

"You are still rich."

"The reason behind my riches is simple — hard work. I poured my efforts into acquiring knowledge, studying relentlessly, and emulating the success of those I admired. If my father had anything to say, he would use his dirty money to corrupt and manipulate me. Using me to his advantage. What kind of parent does that to their child?"

Exactly. What kind of parent!

"Are you saying... you do not work in the family business?"

"I never said that. My brother and I worked in the Bianchi business from the ground up. We made sure to meet and know the employees working alongside with them. After that, I had a life outside the Bianchi business and made my own money because I would not rely on my father and be used and manipulated."

"Well done. You must know I cannot allow you to live."

"Seriously... after everything, you still want me dead. You are unbelievable, lady. What will your sons say to you for murdering me?"

"Not much. My boys will be too busy taking over the family business to worry about you."

"Are you insane? Your sons will not be able to walk in and take over. There have been protocols put in place."

"What protocols?"

"Just as I said."

"I should still shoot you and worry about the finer details later."

"Look, Melissa, you're not catching on... are you?" Dekk pauses long enough to make sure the stupid woman is listening. "If anything happened to my pathetic father outside that of natural death, my father made sure the company and money would be broken up and given to charity. Leo and I would not receive a cent. My father made sure of it in his will."

"What?"

"Well done, Melissa. You destroyed any chance for the Bianchi business to continue."

"But... B. But that cannot be so?"

"Every word is correct. As we speak, you will find my mother and brother are moving out of the family home. Well, evicted, actually. My father was a lowlife who did not care about his family if he was no longer here to give orders."

"Why are you still here, then?"

"As I said, I made my own money. I have my own life and live in the house I own."

"No... No. No. What have I done?"

"Congratulations. You destroyed any chance your sons might have had to become part of the family business. You have now made over two thousand people lose their jobs. I hope you feel proud of your accomplishments."

As soon as Dekk said those words, I knew he had pushed Melissa too far.

I slid the safety off my gun and opened my eyes.

It all happened so fast.

She retrieved a gun from her pocket.

The hospital door opens with a bang. Leo emerged from behind the door, leaping towards Melissa.

In a swift movement, she turns and raises the gun, her focus on Leo.

I didn't wait. With my gun in my hand, I squeeze the trigger. I feel the kickback of my handgun. The bullet rips through the sheet, hitting Melissa in the chest. As the gunfire rings out, the small room becomes filled with the echoing noise. The first thing that catches my attention is how surprised she looks. Next, I witness Leo's descent as he falls to the floor.

Oh, no. The idiot has got himself shot.

A dark bloom forms on Melissa's front. Her eyes grew wide before she glances at my husband. She struggles to lift her gun toward him.

As I push back against Dekk to make him move out of the way of her gun. We both shoot at the same time. Mine is a direct headshot. I'm jolted against Dekk as something sharp rips into my injured shoulder. Pain spreads like wildfire through my body.

In that split second, our eyes connect, and then Melissa's body gives way, collapsing from the chair to the floor with a heavy thud.

My hospital room door barges open again, and I struggle to lift my gun towards the opening as my parents come rushing in. My mother screams something out and is instantly by my side with her gun in her hand.

Gray dots form in front of my vision. White noise penetrates my ears as I mumble Dekk's name. I notice the pain I felt moments before is gone, and the white noise increase just before the room turns black.

Chapter Thirty-Two

DEKK

Not again.

I survey her unconscious body with tubes and wires attached to her and watch her chest gently rise with each breath she takes.

My girl continues to protect me.

How many times can she be shot before she dies?

Once again, I sit in her hospital room, holding her hand, waiting for her to wake up from another surgery.

Because of me! How can I ever forgive myself? I know she will leave me. Who would want to remain married to me?

My beautiful wife. My protector. My bodyguard.

"*D*ekk."

Huh?

"Declyn, wake up," Synn's weak voice penetrates through the sleeping fog, alerting me she is awake.

I sit up, blinking away sleep, and focus on my beautiful wife.

With her hand still in mine, I smile at her gorgeous face.

"Hey, beautiful. Good to see you're awake." I focus on her eyes to see what condition she is in. My wife can be a talented actress, but her eyes usually display how much pain she has. I bet she's thirsty.

I release her hand and stand, reaching for her water jug and the empty glass on the nearby table. "Here, baby, I'll pour you a drink."

Before she speaks, I bring the glass of water to her lips, and she takes a small sip. Then, after a couple more, she nods, and I sit the glass back on the side table.

"Thanks, Dekk. I needed that," she croaks.

"You're welcome, babe. Do you have much pain?"

Her face scrunches in pain when she moves her shoulder. A pained hiss escapes her lips.

Internally, I fight back my anger. Because of my family, she could have died. For Pete's sake, she's on maternity leave and has four bullet wounds to her collection.

Her eyes meet mine. I can see pain radiate through

them. "Dekk, I have been reshot," she states more than she asks.

I nod. "You must stop placing yourself in front of bullets, Synn." I try to smile to let her know I am partly joking. My face turns serious. "Synn, you could have died. I nearly lost you and our children again."

Her hand reaches down to her belly. "Declyn, I will always protect the ones I love," she says with a smile that reaches her eyes. I reach for her hand without the cannula.

"Baby, I love you, too." I hold on tight to her hand. "I have been so worried and scared. I don't know what I would do without you."

With a smile, she says, "Dekk, you're not going to get rid of me that easily."

"I love you," I whisper and lean forward. I brush my lips against hers when a knock sounds on the door. Her parents and sister walk in before I can say anything else.

Great... here we go.

"Essynda, thank goodness. You're awake," Synn's mother, Susanna, says.

"Mother, settle down and allow Essy to breathe," Laini snaps.

I turn my head enough and notice Laini was not happy. I would be annoyed with her parents for keeping the news of her parentage. Laini walks away from her parents and sits on the other side of the bed.

"Hey, Essy. We have sooo much to catch up on."

I turn and watch Synn become uncomfortable. She glances from her parents to her sister, back to her parents, and then back to me.

"Everyone, as good as it is to see you all. Essy has just woken." I reach for the buzzer and press it to notify the nurse. "Her doctor would like to see her."

"Declyn, we only wanted to see Essy and make sure she is okay," Synn's mother, Susanna, exclaims.

"I know, but give her space. We have not spoken of the latest incident... She requires time. Do not rush her."

I meet Synn's eyes and smile. I can tell she is busy thinking. How do you explain to your wife that she shot and killed someone the day before? Knowing her, she will say she was only doing her job, bottling any emotions and feelings she might have.

Chapter Thirty-Three

ESSY

I watch the door close on my parents, relieved I don't have to speak with them — yet. I glance at my sister, and our eyes meet. Yep. The parents have informed her they are our biological parents, and she is overwhelmed by the news. She gives me a small smile and nods before turning, reaching for the door, and leaving.

My sister and I have a lot to talk about. So much to discuss.

"Essy, I'll step outside while the doctor and nurse speak with you." I turn my head enough toward Dekk. I nod at his words and watch him walk out the door. My belly moves as I feel movement from within, reminding me that the twins are awake. Thank goodness they are alive.

I flinch when I suck in a breath, feeling pain radiate from my shoulder. Damn it. I am so over pain right now.

"Mrs. Bianchi, do you have much pain?" the doctor

asks. Duh. I glance at him with a raised eyebrow and nod. "Would you like something for the pain?" Seriously? I have been shot. I have bullet wounds, and he asks if I would like something for the pain.

Save me from incompetence.

I glance over his skinny form of dark smooth skin, short black scruffy hair, and thick black-framed glasses perched on his long nose. He resembles a student wearing his white lab coat two sizes too big. My luck, he probably is.

I survey the room before watching the nurse typing away at the computer terminal. Her eyes would flick up to the different equipment monitors before reading whatever she had on her computer screen.

"When can I go home, Doctor?" I murmur before facing him again. "I don't feel safe here."

The skinny kid doctor takes a step back from the side of the bed and moves towards the computer terminal. After several clicks of the mouse, he faces me with a frown.

"Mrs. Bianchi, it would be wise to spend a minimum of two nights in the hospital. We'll reevaluate after that, providing you can receive proper medical care at your home."

Surely some nurses hire themselves out. I'm safer at my parent's building than I would here. Look how the last incident happened. Melissa, dressed as a nurse with a gun in her pocket, slipped into my room.

"What about my babies, doctor?" I glance between him and the nurse. "How have they been?"

The doctor pulls a face before reading something else on the screen.

"Mrs. Bianchi. Your babies have miraculously escaped harm." Why do I have the feeling there is a big *but* coming... "It is your blood pressure that we have been concerned about." And there it is. The big *but*. I wondered how my blood pressure had been handling all this drama in my life. "We think being released home with your own nurse will reduce your stress." Wow... He doesn't say... I nod to his words in agreement.

"Most likely, Doctor. I would feel more comfortable and safer at home." But, on second thought, I do not want to go back to my parent's home. I wonder if Dekk has his safe house available or maybe his main residence. Of course, it will all depend on where his mother and brother are staying. But then, I have a four-bedroom apartment in the same building as my parents. The last I checked, it was still under construction with significant modifications. Laini would know how my apartment is going. She is handling the decorating.

The skinny kid doctor smiles down at me with a nod of his chin. "Certainly, Mrs. Bianchi. Providing how you go during the next couple of nights, I will reevaluate then."

hen Dekk and I arrived from the hospital three days later, my apartment was

complete and fully furnished, thanks to my genius sister. The annoying doctor insisted on my staying until he was convinced that my blood pressure had dropped enough before leaving the hospital.

I glance around the baby's room that my talented sister decorated. She eagerly bounces on the balls of her feet beside me. Boy, did she create a masterpiece. She has been busy painting the twins' room with a forest scene with gorgeous animals around the walls. I don't know how she did it, but she made it feel like a fairy tale theme instead of scary animals watching your every move.

I wipe my face and clear away the happy tears.

Laini has outdone herself and has done a fantastic job.

I manage to wrap my arm around her. "I love it, Sis. I love it. Thank you so much," I cry, talking into her shoulder. "The babies will love their room." Laini pulls back and wipes her smiling face. Geez, this happy moment stuff is far too hormonal. "You should have become an interior decorator and painter. Your talents are extraordinary."

With a straight face, she replies, "Yeah. I know. I love painting. You got me on a good day."

"A good day... You are bloody talented. Fabulous, Laini."

She grins and shrugs her shoulders. "What can I say?" Laini places her hand on my extended belly. "I love these guys." The movement of the twins jostles her hand, and she lets out a laugh. "See, the little ones love me. I'm lovable."

I laugh as well. My sister is contagious with her laughter. "Yes, you are. Now come here. I need a hug."

We embrace. Laini's warmth soaks through my clothing. Since I have been home from the hospital, we have talked. Talked some more and screamed. Cried and yelled with lots of hugs in between — bloody parents!

Even though we still love our parents, we are both disappointed and annoyed with them. We are happy they'd discovered their lost embryos — alive. But, it does not excuse them from keeping the information from us.

*F*rustrated and annoyed is what I am feeling right now. I could scrunch the A4 pages in my hands into balls and throw them. Instead, I survey the documents containing the last of the information. And now, I have to discuss what I have discovered with my husband — he needs to know the truth.

With Dekk's aunt explaining her version of this so-called family curse, I knew I had to complete my research. Realistically, I do not believe in such a thing. However, Declyn and Leo thought it true, especially when they believed the verbal lies as evidence.

I've reached out. Calling in favors owed to me in the different government departments. I have been determined to complete a thorough family history research for Dekk. My fingers grip the pages harder. Pages I'm relieved to have in my possession. The information arrived twenty minutes ago.

It is time I spoke with Declyn. He will not like it — not one bit. He had been staying with his pain-in-the-butt brother and mother at his coastal house in Amherst Street, New York, and making sure Leo recuperated from his bullet wound to his side. More likely, Leo milks everything he can to earn sympathy and be waited on hand and foot.

Then there is the matter of Mr. Bianchi's written will. Dekk has been busy sorting what he can with the solicitor while their mother keeps interrupting. She does not believe she has lost everything. With my husband staying at his New York house, our time together has become limited.

It's time to contact Dekk and pick up my cell. I need him here by my side at West 48th Street.

Chapter Thirty-Four

DEKK

*V*isions of holding my wife from a couple of days ago before trudging back to my house fill my thoughts. I don't care what my mother demands. If I want to see my wife and spend time with her, I will.

When it comes to my mother, frustration doesn't even cover it. She was insistent on having all my attention for the past week, griping and whining about her financial situation, and specifically how she was not included in my father's will. Maybe she should have learned not to rely on her cheating, low-life husband. Geez. She spent money like she had a never-ending supply, and Dad allowed it.

Thanks to my wife and her observation skills, we discovered my father's hidden safe last week while Mother was on one of her spending sprees. After figuring out how to open the safe door, we discovered a treasure trove of documents, cash, jewelry, land titles, and paperwork related to overseas bank accounts. The discovery of two cell phones made us aware of our father's two mistresses. He had them living in a separate townhouse, which he owned. And by the paper trail, he had traveled extensively with both women to Hawaii and Bali.

My father always had a backup plan. My father thought he'd covered his tracks. But, thankfully, he's not as clever as he had thought. We still found loopholes to salvage the family business and save our employee's jobs.

Mother now has to have a tight leash on her spending, much to her dismay. I told her twenty minutes ago that she should go and get a job if she wanted more spending money. As expected, she did not take the news well, and my ears were still ringing from her high-pitched rant.

My mother expects me to pay for her expenditures and look after her. No way in hell am I going to be her never-ending bank account. There is enough money for her to live a quiet life. Instead, she prefers to keep spending, living it up, and taking her friends out to expensive restaurants. Leo and I have decided it's best to destroy her credit cards. She has to learn. Money does not grow on trees.

"Leo, did the bank agree with you to close Mother's bank account?"

Leo gazes upwards and shakes his head with disdain. "Are you aware that she has an overdraft on her account? The bank manager advised us to have Mother close her account and go to a different bank after learning she had no money."

It doesn't surprise me. I had two other banking

associations say the same thing. Yet, they still demanded that Mother's credit card bills be paid in full or legal action take place. Mother had left her handbag containing her credit cards on the coffee table. After the last phone call to the financial institution, I searched for a sharp pair of scissors.

Plastic pieces of credit cards scatter into the kitchen wastebasket. When I cut up the last of Mother's credit cards, relief fills me.

"Thank goodness I brought in my old college friend to go over Father's will and the pile of paperwork from that safe."

"Mother wanted to remain with Dad's legal solicitor. I don't know why, the guy was ripping us off."

"Yeah, I agree. I was lucky I contacted Geoffrey Holmes. His company had time to look into the estate affairs. We could have lost everything. At least now there is something for the future Bianchi generations."

The phone call from Geoffery early this morning was shocking. Thankfully, we discovered the significant loophole where our fathers' mistresses were concerned. The two women were technically left with nothing once you combed through the fine print of the will. While I sit here, the two women are being handed eviction notices. It is best to sell these houses. We do not require a constant reminder of what our father did.

Little by little, we are learning more about our father. I think our father did not like seeing his brother happy. We're learning our father was jealous of his twin. That is why he had won over our mother from his brother. It goes to show how our mother can be used and manipulated. With his brother dead, our father would claim ownership of the corporation. We are still investigating how our uncle died — we are certain it was at the hands of our father. We just have to prove it.

With a fresh cup of coffee in my hands, I sit down to relax and enjoy my favorite brew. A sigh leaves my lips as I savor each sip. Not even halfway through when my cell chimes with an incoming call. Synn's name appears on the screen, and my first thought — is there's something wrong.

With my heart in my throat, I tap the screen. "Essy. Is everything okay?" I rush out.

"Hello to you, too, Dekk. Geez, take a breath, will ya." I hear her huff down the line. "Yes. We are all okay. Geez, Declyn."

Relief filled me that she and the twins were okay. But, after everything happening over the last month or so, how would I not worry about her? My girl has nearly been killed three times.

Confusion fills me. "Is there something I've forgotten?"

"No, Dekk. I have some news. Grab your annoying brother and bring him over to my place. I'll fill you in on the rest when you both arrive." Feeling nervous, I glance over at Leo. I wonder what her news is?

*W*e arrive at Synn's apartment an hour later. I give Leo a look to shut up. He keeps mumbling under his breath that he has somewhere else to be. Unbelievable, the guy is meant to be recuperating back at my house, not off behaving like a playboy. Oh, there is also the little detail he is legally engaged to Caroline.

We follow Laini and step into the formal lounge area. My heart speeds up when I spot Synn lounging on one of the two matching recliner armchairs with her feet up and drinking from the mug in her hand. Relief fills me. Seeing my wife is not in pain or labor.

I lean down and brush my lips over hers. Heat filled with need and want fills me from the briefest of touches. "Hey, you. Everything okay?" I murmur and gently run over her baby bump, feeling our babe move beneath my hand.

She nods, and with a wave of her hand, Leo and I sit on one of the two black three-seater leather lounges positioned around the carved hardwood coffee table with built-in drawers. My tummy rumbles when I spot the plate of sliced fruit cake. I motioned to Synn if she would like a piece. She shakes her head in no and points for me to take a piece.

With my belly grumbling again, I smile and nod, reach down, and grab a slice and a napkin. The first mouthful causes my mouth to water. Then, within two more bites, the piece is gone. As quickly as the first, I grab another piece, just about swallowing it whole. I reach for another slice, sit back down, glance over the tabletop, and wonder what the two black folders containing several sheets of paper are for.

It is not hard to see Synn is overthinking something as she takes another sip from her favorite coffee cup, knowing she is drinking her favorite herbal tea.

Not sure where this meeting was headed, I began the conversation, keeping my voice as normal as possible, and asked, "Okay, love. Out with it. I know you have something important to say." Synn glances my way before her eyes focus on the folders on the table before she nods to Laini towards the folders.

My sister-in-law soon gets up from her chair and places her and Synn's coffee cups on the table. She picks up the two folders, passing one to Synn and the other to me.

Now I am intrigued. What paperwork has Synn to show me? Surely she will not issue me with divorce papers?

I glance from the folder to Synn. My wife gives me a small smile, then turns her head towards Laini. "Sis, can you make everyone hot drinks, please?"

Laini nods and grabs their cups before walking toward the kitchen.

Synn turns towards me and takes in a breath. "Dekk. I asked both you and," she looks towards Leo, then back to me and tilts her head towards my brother, "Leo, to be here. I have some important information that you both should know."

Leo cuts in before I can say a word. "What news? What is this meeting about, Sweets?"

She glances back and forth between my brother and me.

"I will try to keep this brief. Since leaving the hospital, I have continued researching your family history."

"Okay," I hedge. "What have you discovered?" After what Melissa said about the family curse, I do not know if I can take any more news about my so-called family.

"A lot more than your aunt."

Now my wife has my full attention. What has she discovered?

"What is that supposed to mean?" my brother demands. After he woke up from surgery, I told him what Melissa had said and how this so-called family curse began. He was not impressed with the news.

"I have several documents containing facts contradicting your aunt's claims."

"All right... what are the facts?" I ask, not knowing if I will like the new information.

Synn points towards the folder. "Take a look. Start at the beginning."

I lean forward and open the folder. Bright white pages stare back at me with line after line of black printed writing. I take a breath, glance towards Synn, then back to the page, releasing my breath. Here goes. I read the first paragraph and skimmed over the page, slowly taking in words. The more I read, the more I became shocked. Finally, I glance up, and Synn nods, encouraging me to continue.

It is noted back in the early nineteen hundreds; two brothers created what is now known as the family curse. The same story Melissa had explained to me regarding the two brothers back in the Salem times. They wanted to use this so-called curse to bed women. Manipulating women to believe they are saving the lives of the Bianchi men, causing a string of by-blows to be born. These two men were renowned for organizing secret masked orgies.

There had been no reason for the two brothers to perform the ritual. The men of the Bianchi family have shared the same woman simultaneously or separately for far too many generations. As stated on the page in front of me, they enjoyed a good sex life. The family curse was a sham.

Gobsmacked is a term I would use. How did Synn discover all this information? After several minutes of reading several pages, I glance up at Leo, pass him the pages I've read, and then continue reading the rest of the bundle in the folder.

After a few minutes or so, Leo ruffles the sheets of paper. "Are you serious right now? Is this real?" Leo demands. "We have been lied to. Made to believe there was a real family curse, when in fact there was no curse."

Yes. I read the first page.

Summing up what I have read, each Bianchi family member has died from an accident, sickness, fighting in one of the world wars, or taking one's own life.

The information, including names and dates, also states that several deaths had also been caused by the hand of another family member. Talk about not trusting your family with your life.

I must admit, Leo and I had shared the same woman in our college years. I was extremely hesitant when it came to Synn. But we fell for what our father had said. I believed his words regarding the so-called family curse, and we thought we were running out of time.

One paragraph which caught my eye reminds me of what Melissa mentioned about both brothers impregnating the same woman, resulting in the birth of twins. The last thing I need is for Leo to take it to heart and think Synn's twins belong to both of us. I hope he notices the main paragraph when twins are born; they mainly belong to one brother.

My eyes flicker upward to meet Synn's gaze. Concern was evident in her eyes. With a brief smile, I break eye contact and continue reading the pages. Even though reading these pages eases some concerns, I'm still troubled since meeting Melissa and her sons. Am I the father of Synn's twins, or do they belong to both Leo and me? I hope not. Synn can barely tolerate Leo at the best of times. If my brother turns out to be a father to one twin, help us all. I continue to pass Leo more sheets of the printouts.

"Essy, thank you for looking into the Bianchi family curse." I glance towards Leo, then back to my wife. "I do not want our children to think their lives depend on it."

"Yes, Sweets. Thank you. I do not want our next generation to be dictated by lies," Leo murmurs as he reads through the sheets of paper.

Chapter Thirty-Five

ESSY

*M*y heart understands that Dekk was fooled by his father's meddling and his obsession with the family curse. But the night the three of us slept together, I knew both Dekk and Leo were worried about something. They gave me ridiculous excuses — how a ménage à trois would "save their lives." Please. That's the kind of line men have been feeding women since the dawn of time. As for me, it was my desire to spend the night with Declyn. But then I let myself get swept into their fantasy — the chance of enjoying two men at once, a so-called once-in-a-lifetime experience. It was a moment I never want to relive, an experience I would never wish to repeat. That enigmatic night of passion and wildness, involving his brother, left me feeling more than foolish and used. And let's be honest — nothing screams "romance" like chanting weird family curse words while surrounded by candles like a bad horror movie.

Even after everything that happened, I still honored my agreement for a marriage of convenience with Dekk. We exchanged vows the following morning, basked in eight days of honeymoon ecstasy, and then I was called up — urgent top-secret mission. I set out on a special government assignment. This wasn't some routine FBI gig — it was high-level, classified, and deadly. The days blurred into weeks. My cover was deep, my nerves frayed, and exhaustion weighed me down. I was embedded in a network that made the mob look like kindergarten bullies. Every move had to be calculated, every word rehearsed. I was collecting information that could topple powerful people, and I knew if I slipped, I'd be dead. On the last day of the mission, just as I was securing the final piece of intel, something went wrong.

I was attacked. The ambush came from all sides, leaving me with the horrifying realization that I was betrayed and I was dead. The air filled with deafening blasts of gunfire, muzzle flashes lighting up the night like fireworks from hell. A wave of agonizing pain washed over me as bullets tore into my body. Then the bastards tossed me into the bone-chilling river. Fantastic, right? Nothing says "job well done" like being used for target practice and dumped like trash. Somehow, before losing consciousness, I managed to activate my locating beacon. My fingers were numb, my vision fading, but muscle memory saved me. Thankfully, two of my fellow undercover FBI agents found me floating down the rapids, snagged against a thick tree limb. They freed me from the sharp branches and freezing water, calling in a medical unit. I was half-frozen, half-dead, and fully pissed off.

When I opened my eyes, a stranger sat at my bedside. Weeks had passed since my admission to the ICU. The stranger turned out to be my doctor. He explained my injuries, how lucky I was to be alive, and then dropped the bombshell — I was pregnant. Pregnant. After surviving bullets and rivers, now I had two tiny passengers along for the ride. As an FBI agent, discovering I was pregnant was my turning point. My babies became my focus. I decided to resign from the FBI and turn my security business into a full-time occupation. Because apparently, dodging bullets and being tossed into rivers isn't the best prenatal care plan. After a couple more weeks, I was transferred to another hospital, then finally to my sister's beach house to recuperate.

While recovering, I realized it was time to dig deeper into the Bianchi family's medical history for my twins. And with Dekk silent, I needed to investigate my husband too. Had he moved on? Was there still a chance for a genuine marriage? So I began my research. And let me tell you, nothing says "romantic marriage" like Googling your husband to see if he's still alive or just hiding. How I hate the tabloids and those photoshopped photographs with fake stories.

And now, months later, here I am — living with my husband in my apartment, due to deliver our twins any day. Don't even get me started on Leo and his idiotic attempt to come between us, demanding a paternity test. I feel in my heart the twins belong to Dekk. But for some stupid reason, Leo is confident one twin belongs to him. Honestly, the man acts like he's auditioning for a daytime soap opera.

Chapter Thirty-Six

ESSY

y heart swells as I cradle my twin boys, their tiny bodies warm and impossibly fragile against my chest. Their breaths come in soft, uneven rhythms, little sighs that make me ache with love. I can't stop staring at them — two perfect faces, two sets of miniature fingers curled tight as if they already know how to hold on.

Two hours ago, I asked the doctor to take blood and saliva samples. DNA testing. Cold, clinical, necessary. I want this paternity mess dealt with quickly. In my soul, I know Dekk is their father, but I need proof. Proof to silence Leo, proof to protect my boys. I refuse to let doubt hover over us like a storm cloud.

Last night feels like pandemonium stitched together with adrenaline. One moment I was finishing dinner, then suddenly my waters broke, and contractions hit me like kook waves, all sixty feet high and powerful. I told Dekk not to call anyone until the twins arrived.

I can laugh about it now, but last night he practically

dragged me out the door, his hand gripping mine as if he was afraid I'd vanish. He drove like a man possessed, eyes flicking between the road and me, torn between excitement and sheer terror. I couldn't tell if he was more thrilled that the boys were finally coming or shitting himself that fatherhood was about to hit him hard. Probably both.

Now the hospital hums around me — nurses moving briskly, machines beeping, the faint antiseptic sting in the air. Lunch has come and gone, and I'm still starving. The food here is bland, forgettable, but I don't care. My boys are bathed, fed, and sleeping peacefully, their tiny chests rising and falling in perfect rhythm. Every time I try to get up for a shower, one of them stirs, and I stay rooted, watching. My body aches, my hair is a mess, but none of it matters. My chest aches with pride. I'm a mother. The word feels unreal, heavy, miraculous.

The shutter click of Dekk's phone keeps breaking the silence. He's relentless, crouched beside me, snapping photo after photo like a man obsessed.

I arch a brow at him, voice dry. "Dekk, how many more pictures are you going to take?"

His grin is boyish, almost disbelieving. "Synn, look at them. I can't believe they're ours."

I glance down at the boys, smiling despite myself. "I know exactly what you mean."

But he doesn't stop. Hundreds of photos already, and still going. Time to redirect. "Dekk, I've been thinking. Let's keep the details about their distinguishing marks to ourselves."

He nods, fingers brushing Frazer's head, tracing the

curve of his ear with a tenderness that makes my throat tighten. "Agreed. Frazer's ears are a little different, but who knows if that'll last."

"The permanent difference is the birthmarks," I remind him. "Frazer's on his right butt cheek, Bryon's on his shoulder. Both shaped like hearts. It's uncanny."

Dekk chuckles, shaking his head. "Give it time. When they're teenagers, they'll probably tattoo over them."

I laugh softly, exhaustion mixing with amusement. "You think so?"

"I know so."

I must have dozed off. The bed dips, and my eyes snap open to find Dekk sitting there, grinning like he's just won the lottery. His smile is so wide it practically splits his face.

"Hey, Synn. Have I told you lately I love you and our two boys?"

My lips twitch at his words. Typical Dekk — sentimental one moment, smug the next. I glance down at our sleeping sons, their tiny fists curled against their cheeks, their breaths soft and uneven. It might be time to place them in their cribs, as hard as it is to let them go. My body screams for another shower; I can feel the hospital sweat clinging to me.

"Yes, you have, my husband. Now be useful and put

Frazer and Bryon in their cribs. I should shower before we phone the family."

Dekk frowns, hesitation flickering across his face. His eyes dart between me and the boys, like he's weighing whether to argue.

"What is it, Dekk?"

"I've been enjoying our time together without the hassle of our family."

I sigh, because he's right. It has been peaceful. No stress, no interference, just us and the boys. The quiet feels sacred. "Yes, it's been blissfully stress-free. But it's time to contact your mother and my parents. They've been itching to know when I go into labor."

Dekk flinches, guilt flashing in his eyes. "They won't be pleased to discover the boys are here. And that they missed the birth."

I shake my head, firm. "Stiff. The boys belong to us. We are their parents. Our parents, as new grandparents, will need to learn to take a back seat and back off."

Bugger. Bryon picks up on my tension and fusses, his little mouth twisting as he whimpers. Dekk scoops up Frazer with practiced ease, while I settle Bryon against my breast. He latches instantly, suckling himself back into sleep. The relief that floods me is instant — the rhythm of his feeding calms my nerves as much as it calms him.

"Dekk, you know what? Instead of phoning our parents, call Laini. Ask her to bring me a mixed chicken salad with a slice of apple pie and cream from the bakery near my apartment. Tell her I said, 'Mum's the word.' She'll know to keep quiet."

Dekk places Frazer in the crib, his movements careful, reverent. He reaches for Bryon next, his big hands surprisingly gentle.

"Will Laini inform your parents?"

"Nah. That's why you must say those exact words. She'll understand." He burps Bryon in seconds. How does he do that? The little bugger never burps that fast for me.

"Okay. I can do that. You should shower. The boys and I will stay here and have some male bonding time." He places Bryon in his crib, stroking his head with a tenderness that makes my chest ache.

"Dekk, ask Laini to grab you something to eat too."

He nods, eyes locked on our boys, already lost in them. His whole body softens as he watches them, like the weight of the world has shifted.

I linger a moment longer, watching the three of them together — my husband, my sons — before dragging myself toward the bathroom. The sound of Dekk humming under his breath follows me, low and steady, a lullaby meant more for himself than the boys.

*A*fter my much-needed shower, I feel human again. My hair is damp, twisted into a messy bun, and clean pajamas cling to my skin. Steam still clings to me, the faint scent of hospital soap mixing with the sterile air. I step out to find Laini perched on my bed, smiling wide, while Dekk devours food like he hasn't eaten in days.

I mouth, Thank you. She nods knowingly, her eyes sparkling with mischief.

"Hello, new momma," Laini sings softly, wrapping me in a hug that nearly squeezes the breath out of me. "Why didn't you call earlier?"

"With all the Braxton Hicks contractions lately, I wasn't about to interrupt your evening for another false alarm," I mumble against her ear.

"I wouldn't have minded. But I'm glad you didn't. Mom and Dad were with me at the gala dinner for the magazine fundraiser."

Relief washes through me. The gala was the last thing on my mind. "Ahh. How did last night go? I'm sorry. I forgot all about it."

"No problem. When you didn't answer our usual text, I figured something was happening. I told Mom and Dad you were suffering from heartburn. You've had plenty of that."

"Thanks." And I mean it. Laini always senses things. At least she kept our parents from blowing up my phone.

"You're welcome. I was waiting for your call this morning." She turns to the boys, her smile softening. "Sis, they're gorgeous. I can't wait to hold them."

"Don't speak too soon. They'll wake and show you how loud they can get."

My stomach growls. Hospital food is a crime against humanity. Laini tucks me into bed, wheels the little table over, and I dive into the chicken salad, followed by most of the apple pie.

"Hey... Aren't you going to share that?" Dekk teases, eyes gleaming.

I glance at the last two bites, sigh, and scoop up a forkful. He's beside me in seconds, mouth open like a kid. I feed him, then lift the last bite. He grins, swallows, and waits.

"Wow," Laini gasps. "My sister never shares her pie. Not with me, anyway."

Dekk winks. "What can I say? My wife loves me."

He's right. I wouldn't share with just anyone. I do love him.

He mouths I love you, then kisses me senseless. His mouth tastes of apple pie, and I almost chase his tongue for that last sweet bite.

A knock interrupts us. Damn. I was enjoying that.

The doctor enters, folder in hand. My pulse spikes. DNA results. She hesitates, glancing at Laini.

"This is my sister," I explain quickly. Laini smiles, excuses herself, and slips out, closing the door behind her. Clever girl.

*T*he doctor faces us, folder tucked under her arm, her expression careful. My pulse spikes. DNA results.

She opens the folder, pulls out the sheet, and

exhales. "Because Declyn and Leo are identical twins, standard paternity tests couldn't distinguish between them. Identical twins share almost all of their DNA — the usual fifteen to twenty genetic markers we test are identical in both men. In cases like this, the results would normally come back inconclusive."

My stomach knots. I glance at Dekk, his jaw tight, his hand gripping mine.

The doctor continues, her tone steady but serious. "To resolve this, we had to use whole genome sequencing. That means scanning all six billion DNA letters, searching for rare differences — tiny mutations that make Declyn's DNA unique from Leo's. It's technically challenging, and not something we do often. But those differences are what allowed us to reach a conclusion."

She passes me the paper, then looks at Dekk. "Long story short, the test proves Declyn is ninety-nine percent the father of your sons."

My brain stalls. Ninety-nine percent. Proof.

"Congratulations, Declyn. You are the biological father."

Relief floods his face, his shoulders sagging as if a weight has finally lifted. He kisses me hard, then moves to our boys, pressing kisses to their heads.

I watch him, my chest aching with joy. The tension that's been gnawing at me dissolves. The doctor's words echo in my head — rare differences, technically challenging, ninety-nine percent. Proof that Leo can't touch us now.

Dekk turns back, his voice rough. "One thing I want to know. How did you get Leo's DNA?"

The doctor leans against the bed, her expression calm. "Yesterday, your brother had follow-up blood tests. His samples were still in our lab. We used them for comparison."

Ha. I would've guessed his blood work was for STDs.

I clutch the paper tighter, the black letters blurring as tears prick my eyes. My boys are Dekk's. Ours. No one can take that from us.

I lean into him, whispering so only he hears. "Leo's done. He can't touch us now."

Dekk exhales, a shaky laugh escaping. "He never could. But now we've got proof."

I glance at our boys, sleeping soundly in their cribs, unaware of the storm that's just passed. My heart swells. For the first time since last night, I feel peace.

Chapter Thirty-Seven

ESSY

With the paternity out of the way, Dekk and I completed the boy's birth registry documentation and had Laini witness each form. The doctor also fills in her part and signs and takes her copy so she can lodge it with the hospital.

After several photos are taken, I begin to yawn. "Are you guys able to lodge the paperwork for the boy's birth?" I yawn again, struggling to keep my eyes open.

The pressure of warm lips on my forehead lets me know Dekk is beside me.

"Synn, I want you to sleep for an hour or so. That should give Laini and me enough time to lodge the birth documents. Then I will phone our parents."

My sister's voice quietly tickles my ears. "Sleep, Sis. We will be back before you know it. I'll bring tea, coffee, and some snacks." I nod at her words and yawn again.

Before the door closes behind them, I am out.

*S*omeone is stroking my head as I wake. An action my mother used to do when I was a child sleeping.

I open my eyes to find Dekk, Laini with my parents, and Dekk's mother in my room. I sit up and smile. Wow! I slept longer than I had expected.

"Hello, everyone," I say, stretching and noting that both my boys are sleeping soundly in their cribs.

The sound of a knock at the door caused everyone to turn. Leo bursts in, laden with an enormous bouquet and two large stuffed teddy bears.

Oh, shit. Not now. Runs through my mind and I meet Dekk's eyes. With a quick nod, he gets up and approaches his brother. Dekk grabs the two teddies and passes them to my sister, then turns back to his brother.

"Hey, Leo. How about we place these flowers in some water?"

Leo shakes his head and attempts to sidestep Dekk.

Dekk grabs Leo's arm and spins him back towards the door.

"Hey. I want to meet the twins," Leo demands.

"My sons are sleeping, Leo. You will not wake them," Dekk growls.

The door closes behind Dekk and Leo with a click. Their agitated voices can be heard through the closed door and gradually become faint.

Good. Dekk is moving them away. We do not require

our parents to listen to what my husband has to say. My thoughts then turn to the DNA results and whether Dekk is carrying the paperwork with him. I am relieved I had requested a copy to be emailed to me, as I can imagine Leo destroying our copy.

As I watch over the twins sleeping, my mother and Matilda continue to ask questions regarding the birth. None the wiser of the turmoil happening out in the corridor.

Leo is going to be devastated. Hopefully, he will take the news of the twins' paternity and remember that the family curse does not exist, and that Dekk is the twins' father.

Chapter Thirty-Eight

DEKK

"What the heck, Declyn?" Leo shrugs my hand off his arm and steps away, leaving me with the flowers.

I observe him. I know the look he has, and it is not good.

"Leo, we need to talk."

He scowls at me. "Yeah, damn right we do." He glances back towards Essy's room and attempts to sidestep me. "Right after you get out of my way. I need to see my son."

I shake my head and reach for him again, preventing Leo from entering the room.

"Come on, bro, we need to discuss a couple of things."

He pauses, and his eyes narrow. "What is going on, Dekka?" I sigh and encourage him to walk away from Synn's room. "Is there something wrong with one of the twins?"

I shake my head. "No, Leo. Both twins are healthy. I

thought it would be best to discuss the boy's paternity away from our mother."

He looks me straight in the eye. "Look, Dekka. Mother will be shocked to discover her sons have both fathered a child."

I shake my head again. "No, Leo. That is just it." A nurse I have seen previously approaches us.

"Hi. Can you place these flowers in some water?" I smile, making sure my dimples show. For some reason, it used to turn the girls on.

The nurse smiles and blushes. Then reaches for the flowers. "Certainly. They are beautiful. I'll be back shortly."

"Thank you."

As I turn, I notice two empty chairs, just up ahead against the wall, and I turn back towards Leo, giving him a nod and gesturing towards them. Once we both sit, I say, "The twins belong to me."

He shakes his head. "What, no. That cannot be right."

"Yes, it can be, Leo. Essy had a DNA test performed after the birth. The doctor informed us of the news not that long ago." I reach into my jacket, pull out a copy of the DNA results, and pass them to Leo. "Here. Read this."

He snatches the documentation and begins to read. "No. This cannot be true. I am one of the fathers — the ceremony," he murmurs as he scans the document.

"No, Leo. Frazer and Bryon are both my sons. I'm sorry, bro. I know how much you wanted a son."

He glances up from the paperwork to my face. "No,

Dekka. I want another DNA test performed. How do I know this one has not been forged?"

"Are you saying I'm lying about the tests? That the doctor forged the results?"

"Yes. That is exactly what I am saying." Leo nods to his words. He is thinking of something. "I want my own DNA test performed. I do not trust Essy or her doctor."

I squeeze my fists beside me and reach for the sides of my chair to prevent myself from thumping my selfish, jealous brother.

"How dare you, Leo! My wife ensured the DNA test was performed as quickly as possible, so you would not be wondering for days if either of my sons were yours." That's it. It is taking everything in me to keep control and not hit him, so I stand and step away. "I think it will be best if you do not return to the room. I do not want you anywhere near my sons or wife. Until you can act and behave like an adult. Leave, Leo."

Before I allow myself to say something I might regret, I turn and storm off toward my wife's room.

How dare Leo instigate Synn would have the DNA results fabricated?

"Brother, I will have my DNA test done. I will prove that I am the father," he says to my back.

I don't stop. I keep my mouth shut and keep walking toward Synn's door.

I take in several deep breaths before entering Synn's room.

My mother notices Leo is not with me. "Declyn, where is Leo?"

I glance towards my sons, then to Synn. She catches

my eye, and I shake my head in warning. She needs to have the heads up. Leo is going to cause trouble.

"Mother, Leo has an appointment to attend and has to leave."

"Will he be back later?" Not if I can help it.

"Most likely." I glance around the room and smile at everyone. "What do you think of the boys?" Attempting to change the subject.

Chapter Thirty-Nine

ESSY

I don't know how he did it, but my husband has kept his annoying brother away from our boys and me. This should be the happiest time of our lives with our newborn sons. But instead, we are on tenterhooks because Leo will not believe the results. I cannot believe my brother-in-law's stupidity.

"Dekk, I think we should arrange with a solicitor to organize the DNA tests. My stress levels are rising, and the twins are picking up on it."

Dekk turns and faces me. I can see the anguish Leo is causing him. Finally, he nods, steps forward, and reaches for my hand, and I place mine in his.

"I think it is time, Essy. My brother has become too much for me. I might love him, but his antics push me over the edge." I know exactly what he means. We have to stop Leo before he does something stupid.

I survey the intimate, friendly, family-run Italian restaurant with envy. My stomach rumbles once more from the delicious odors from the kitchen make my mouth water. If only we could eat here every day.

"Synn, I cannot wait for our food to arrive. My mouth is watering," Dekk eagerly says, watching the kitchen door. "I don't know about you, but I miss our boys."

I nod. I can't shake this uneasy feeling, even though I know our boys are safe with the sitter. After a morning filled with appointments, our six-week check-up came and went. The boys' pediatrician, after a thorough checkup, declared them healthy and gave both boys the all clear, much to our relief. He was pleased to see the twins had gained weight and had a small growth spurt. As for me, the doctor said I could be intimate with Dekk again — something the pair of us have been eagerly waiting for. It has been six long weeks since the birth. Well longer regarding sex, as it became far too uncomfortable near the end of the pregnancy.

"Dekk, have you noticed you have been calling me Synn to my face again?" My husband glances down, his checks pinking up. My lips twitch. "If I remember correctly, you said you only say Synn in your head," I mention with a straight face.

He lifts his head, his eyes smoldering, as his lips

twitch before turning into a full smile. "Let me put it this way, my sexy temptress. When I look at you, my heart bursts with love. As for my love for you, it grows each day we're together," he smiles and lifts his brow. His voice becomes husky, "And I thank the gods in the universe that you, my gorgeous, sexy wife, are sinfully mine and most of all that you're still sin in my bed."

Before I could reply with a witty comeback, Mrs. d'Alessi delivered our plates of steaming beef lasagna with a side salad and a basket of garlic bread. Her cheerful face was glowing, displaying her big, toothy grin and bright red lips.

The woman of sixty years still had the figure of a forty-year-old model. Her eyes rove over my husband and cheekily flirt with him. The cheeky woman winks at me with a saucy grin, letting me know she was only playing. Then she asks in thick Italian, "How are your new bambinos? If they take after their papa, they must be gorgeous."

With a smile and a shake of my head at her words, I proudly say, "The twins are great. I cannot believe how much they have grown already."

She smiles with happiness shining in her eyes. "Give them a kiss and hug. Buon appetito."

We say, "Thank you. We will." I glance down at my plate and breathe in the rich flavors of Italian herbs, spices, tomato, and garlic, causing my mouth to water.

We lifted our cutlery and dug in, literally inhaling our food, enjoying every mouthful with groans of pleasure. The taste was superb.

As I take my last forkful of food, I shiver for no

particular reason — a feeling of foreboding spreads through me.

I glance at my husband. As our eyes meet, he asks, "What is it?"

I shake my head. "I don't know, Dekk. Something is wrong."

I glance around the restaurant, not noticing anything out of the ordinary. I was about to shake it off when the twins came to my mind.

The twins. Oh, no.

"Dekk. Phone the babysitter."

Dekk nods, places his cutlery down, and reaches for his cell phone.

After several seconds, I watched his face change with worry. "No one is answering. I'll try the apartment number."

Without waiting, I reach for my cell and dial my parents.

"Hello, Essynda. How was your dinner?" my mother queried.

"Mom, we're still at the restaurant. Can you go to my apartment? The babysitter is not answering her cell."

I was expecting her to criticize me for panicking for no reason. But instead, she replies, "What is going on, Essynda?"

"That is what I would like to know. Something is wrong. I can feel it."

"Okay, baby girl." I hear a door close and the elevator ding through the speaker.

Dekk signals for Mrs. d'Alessi to bring the bill over.

I stand up, reaching for my large clutch and jacket from the back of my chair, and continue to listen to my mother's progress through my cell speaker. The elevator dings again, indicating she is close to my apartment.

I quietly hear Mrs. d'Alessi speaking with Dekk as I shrug into my jacket.

My mother's mumbled words have me moving toward the door. "Ah, shit. This is not good."

I pause in mid step. "What is it? Speak to me, Mom," I demand.

Dekk is soon beside me, urging me towards our car.

"Ah, Essynda."

Why isn't the woman explaining what is happening? "What do you see, Mom?"

She pauses too long for my liking before replying, "Are you on your way home?"

I held off my smart-ass remark, ready to burst from my lips. "Yes. We are about to climb into the car."

"Essynda, I am placing you on hold and calling your father. Your front door is ajar, and there is no sign of anyone."

I don't know whether to feel scared or angry right now. "What do you mean, there is no sign of anyone?" Dekk gasps. I cannot look at him right now in case I break down. I need to remain strong and to know what is happening. "Check all the rooms," I scream before the line goes silent. Damn it. Mother has placed me on hold.

Somehow, I do not remember clicking my seat belt in or my husband getting into the car. Dekk had our vehicle in motion, speeding towards home, when my mother spoke with me again.

"Essynda, your father is coming over. I have also called for the paramedics." What? Paramedics. What has happened? My mother's voice grabs my attention. "The babysitter is unconscious in the bathroom. It looks like she has an injury to her head. There is blood."

Oh, my god. What has happened inside my home?

"What about the twins, Momma? Where are my babies?"

"Essynda, the boys are not here," her words sound, but I do not want to acknowledge them because what she says can't be true. My world will end if it is.

I don't know if to scream or hit something. No, no, no. This cannot be happening. I turn towards Dekk.

He glances at me before looking back at the road.

"What is happening, Essy?" he demands.

I shake my head, feeling something wet sliding down my cheek. I lift my hand to my face. "Our boys are missing. The babysitter is bleeding and unconscious in the bathroom."

"Shit. What do you mean, the boys are missing? How did the babysitter end up in the bathroom? What about the twins?"

"I don't know, Dekk. Someone has taken our boys. They are not in the apartment."

Before I can say another word, Dekk races into the parking garage of my apartment. "Momma, are you still there?"

"Yes, Essynda. Your father has arrived. He is doing a complete sweep of the apartment, looking for clues."

At least, that is something. Dekk brings the car to a stop in our allocated parking spot. We exited the car and raced to the elevator.

"Momma, we are about to enter the elevators. We will be there in a moment." Dekk had the floor number pushed when I thought of something else. "Momma, call building security. I want the surveillance footage."

"Okay. I'll dial now," she responds. "We'll see you soon."

The elevator doors close, and we begin to move. My foot taps to its own nervous beat. What in the world has happened? Who would do something like this?

Then, it occurs to me. I glance towards Dekk. "Babe, I think I know who has taken the boys. But I want to check the security footage first."

"You think it was Leo."

I nod. "Yes."

He sighs and shakes his head. "I thought you would say that. I have the same feeling."

Chapter Forty

ESSY

*M*inutes pass when my father rushes back through our front door with his laptop, followed by two FBI agents I have not seen in a long time.

"Essy, I am going to set up over here." I nod and reach for Dekk's hand. "I have a live feed recorded on my laptop for the last two hours."

I glance at Dekk. He seems as anxious as I do. I wrap my arms around my husband and press my lips to the side of his head. Leo is going to pay for this.

I pull away from Dekk and face my father. "Dad, what can I do?"

He says over his shoulder, "It will be another minute or so until I am set up." He continues to pull equipment out of his case. "Why don't you get changed and prepare to leave."

I nod and head for my bedroom. As I reach the door, I look over my shoulder at my husband. "Dekk, come and get changed."

I don't wait for him to follow, knowing when my father says to be prepared to leave, be ready for anything. I finish up in the bathroom and come face-to-face with Dekk.

"Do not leave me, Synn." His eyes swarm with tears. One blink, and they will fall. We wrap our arms around one another. "If Leo has our children, he will regret his actions," he hisses.

I agree. Just wait until I find my so-called brother-in-law. "Dekk, I'm not going anywhere without you. As for your brother, he will not get away with this."

Movement over Dekk's shoulder is the only sign that my sister has arrived. Laini's fair hair comes closer into view as she races toward me.

Laini plows into us with an oomph and wraps her arms around us. "Oh, my god. I am going to shoot Leo. How dare he take my nephews? When do we leave?" my sister demands.

My sister might have worked at a high-class glossy woman's magazine, but never get in the way of something she loves — Laini becomes bloodthirsty and has the skills to do it.

*A*djusting the breast pump, I continue to express breast milk. My sister knocks and walks in, shutting the door behind her with the spare bottles.

"Here. These are the last four bottles you have

sterilized." And places them on the little table beside me and sits on the opposite chair.

"Thanks, Laini." I adjusted the breast pump, glanced up, and noticed my sister was lost in thought.

Something is bugging me about my old FBI partner, Jaxton. Why is he here? We met as teenagers in the special children's FBI program. We worked well together for many years until he left suddenly and moved to another division. To another state, if I remember right. It seems he's been hanging around my sister since he arrived. Then it clicks.

"Hey, Laini," I casually say.

Laini looks up from the floor and meets my eyes. "Yes, Essy."

I glance towards the door, making sure it is still closed. "I have a question."

She nods and encourages me to ask. "What's the question?"

"What is going on between you and Jaxton?"

Her eyes widen, and I swear she goes pale. She quickly glances at the door and then back at me. "I don't know what you're speaking about!"

I lower my voice a little more. "Laini, I have seen how you and Jaxton look at one another. I swear you two have an old history. I want to know, was it serious? Do I need to rearrange his face?"

An old memory comes to mind, and then it occurs to me — Jaxton left before Laini went away in what everyone was told was her gap year. Nah...but the timing...Hmm. Could Jaxton be...

I ask in a hushed tone. "Is Jaxton Emma's father?"

She gasps, her face pales again, and she shakes her head in denial. "I don't know what you're speaking of, Essy."

I glance back towards the door. "Come on. Please don't deny it. All I want to know is Jaxton, your daughter's father?"

My sister's eyes mist up before a lone tear rolls down her cheek.

I lean over and wrap my arm around her. "Hey. I am not judging you. I just wish you had said something. Does Jaxton know he is a father?"

I feel Laini nod before pulling away from me. "Yes. Jaxton found out about our daughter a couple of months ago. There was an emergency. Emma's appendix had to come out. The hospital had contacted both of us when there were complications."

"Oh, Laini, why didn't you tell me? I would have been there for you. I wondered what was wrong a couple of months ago when you left for an unexpected business meeting. Is my niece recovered? Is Em okay?"

She nods and wipes her face free of tears. "Yes. But Emma's heart had stopped. It turns out she cannot tolerate the anesthetic. At least the surgeon got her appendix out before her heart stopped."

This time, it was my turn to gasp. "Oh, my gods, Laini. What you must have gone through."

"I stayed by her side until she was well enough to go back to her home."

"Laini, I would have been there if I had known."

My sister shakes her head. "No. Essy, just no. I

would not have you traveling on planes in your condition. You did not require the extra stress."

"What about Mr. and Mrs. Clayton? Were they there at the hospital?"

"Yes. Even though they're Emma's paid careers, they still care for and love my daughter. They remained at the hospital until I sent them home. They needed rest."

"What did Jaxton say about Emma?" Wow. The guy must have been shocked to see Laini and an unknown little girl.

"He wanted to know why the hospital was phoning him."

"Really. So Jaxton never suspected he might be the father?"

"No. When Jaxton saw me sitting beside our daughter, he wanted to know why I was at the hospital." She shook her head, lost in thought. "I told him to leave."

"Wow."

"Yeah. Wow. The guy was about to say something when his cell rang. It was his wife!"

Hang on… "What? Since when is he married?"

"Since — not long after — he got me pregnant."

I stop, holding the machine's tank of milk. "You got to be kidding me. I didn't know Jaxton was married. Are you saying he was unfaithful to both you and the other woman?" I keep filling the bottles.

"No. It turns out his parents arranged his marriage. They didn't like me, Essy. Believe it or not, Jaxton is getting divorced now that his father is dead."

"What…?"

"Jaxton was made to move away when his parents discovered he was seeing me. He had been unsuccessful in getting out of his engagement. According to him, he and his wife have no children. His wife has a lover and spends most of her time with the so-called man instead."

"Oh, my god, Laini. If you tried, you could not have thought up a better plot for one of your steamy romance books."

"Shhhh. Be quiet," Laini hisses. "Our parents do not know about my writing career. And I want to keep it that way."

"Keep your underwear on, will ya? I will not tell them. I promised you I would keep it a secret."

The fridge door is carefully closed, enclosing the little bottles of expressed milk for my precious boys. With my breasts emptied of milk, and the tight fullness gone. I slip two nursing pads inside my bra cups. I've learned to use the nursing pads or ruin another top. The last thing I need is breast milk seeping into my leathers.

It does not take long to change into my trademark black leathers, right down to the solid-heeled boots I was renowned for. I glance at my reflection, clipping the last buckle to my weapon holster. I feel ready to track down my babies with two guns, four throwing stars, and two knives.

Before I hear my husband, I see him in the mirror. I turn to his gasp and groan. I watch his hand adjust his crotch before he steps toward me. "Synn, how am I meant to concentrate with you looking all," his hand waves in front of my body, "sexy? You are gorgeous and ready for sin. If our children were safe, I would pick you up and take you to bed."

My husband. The romantic! I lean forward and wrap my arms around him. "Dekk, I request a raincheck." And smile into his neck, placing a light kiss there. I inhale his scent and step back, dropping my arms by my sides. "Come on. We have a lot of work and little time to do it in." I walk by him and back out to the lounge area. The first thing I see is my family hunched over computers with phones pressed to their ears.

When my father notices me, he says something to his cell, ends the call, and stands. "Essy, we are set."

Chapter Forty-One

ESSY

My father, having organized four vehicles, takes the driver's seat of one and instructs me to get in with him.

Dad verified that Leo, along with his supposed fiancée, had abducted the twins. Security cameras caught them both with my children. Any feelings I once had for my brother-in-law have completely vanished. I am extremely angry with Leo. What was his reason for doing this?

With my emotions overwhelming, I'm thankful my father didn't get me to drive when I notice my hands shake. I'm terrified for my children, to be honest. My sister sits beside me, keeping her cool persona in place, and loads her gun and mine. My husband sits in the front, speaking to my father, going back over details and where Leo was last located.

"Leo's fiancée's a bitch. How dare she take the twins?" Laini murmurs. "What does Leo see in her?" My heart pounds, thumping against my ribs, and my palms sweat. I need to come up with another distraction, or I'm going to lose it and scream my head off.

I glance toward my sister, my eyes meeting hers, and reply to her snarky comment, "When I see her, I'll make sure to ask. If I don't shoot her first."

Laini's lips twitch as she tries to keep a straight, serious face. "Nah. Just shoot her and Leo."

Thanks to my sister, I barely stop myself from laughing. "As tempting as that is, I have to spare Leo for now."

With a pout, Lain asks, "Why? I wouldn't." Now, this is why I love my sister. She knew I needed to banter like this. Even though what we face is serious, she still can make me loosen up and laugh and help me through my rising stress.

While I keep my face serious, I struggle not to laugh and shrug. "He is my husband's twin, after all."

Our father's voice interrupts our conversation. We freeze as if we have been caught in the cookie jar with our hands. "What are you two talking about back there?" Laini shakes her head. I nod at her unspoken words.

"Daddy, are we nearly there?"

Laini shakes her head and nods. "Yeah, Daddy. Are we nearly there?"

I cover my mouth to prevent myself from laughing out loud. If Dad heard me talking about shooting Leo and Caroline, he would refuse to let me get out of the car.

"Really... girls? Do you think I do not know when you're pretending to be speaking of something else?"

"Like what, Dad? Leo and his girlfriend will not get away with taking my children."

Laini elbows me and mouths, "Stop it."

Dad mumbles something. I swear I hear him say, "Just wait until I see him." The car slows down and turns into a side street. Then, louder, he states, "Look, girls. We are here. Keep alert. And don't do anything stupid."

Laini and I look at one another and reply, "Who, us?" And burst out laughing. It was one of Dad's old sayings, since Laini and I were teenagers.

"Girls, I am serious," he demands.

"Yes, Dad. We will keep our wits about us," I drawl.

Chapter Forty-Two

DEKK

The second we stepped out of the cars, the mischievous glint in Synn's eyes told me, without a doubt, that she and her sister had cooked up something. In my peripheral vision, I spot Laini taking a bag out of the car's trunk. When she unzips the bulky bag, she pulls out a heavy object — is that body armor? She tosses me a vest; the buckles clinking as it lands against my chest, before slipping her arms into another and securing the front straps.

These two girls have come prepared for danger. Glad they're on my side.

Without being told, I follow suit, the synthetic fabric of the bulletproof vest rubbing against my cotton long-sleeved t-shirt as I put it on. My wife fills my mind once again as my hand pats my thigh. Her spare leg harness strapped tight around my leg containing the cold steel of the handgun Synn made me take, pressing against my leg an obvious heavy reminder of its presence.

The stupid antics Leo's caused over the years cross my mind. He did not care about the consequences of the different stunts and games he was involved in and expected me to pick up the pieces every time. Whatever he thinks he is up to, this will be one situation I will not be getting him out of.

If the worst-case scenario happens, I'm conflicted. I do not want to shoot my brother, but I will kill him if he hurts or injures my kids. Once again, he is showing how selfish he is.

Wow, we don't require a family curse, especially when we have selfishness and stupidity in the family — no wonder the men in my family die if they have been pulling stupid stunts similar to this.

Standing against an old hotel brick wall, I wonder what we are doing here. Surely Leo wouldn't stay here? But then again, he is attempting to keep a low profile. Of course, he would think of something like this. Idiot. See, once again, he is not thinking things through.

It is not long before Synn signals for me to follow her. She taps her ear and smiles at me. We might be in danger, but her smile still affects me straight to my groin. I know that both she and Laini are wearing earpieces, keeping them updated, most likely from their mother in the control van, and yet I am denied one of those tiny earbuds to go into my ear.

"Honey, I need you to stay by my side. Got it!" my gorgeous wife says with a straight, serious face. Okay, it's her — Don't mess with me and do as your told face. I nod and move closer, keeping in time with her steps.

"Where are Laini and that guy... Jaxton going?"

Synn glances over her shoulder towards me, then scans the area before walking forward again. "Laini and Jaxton have their orders. I need you to keep focused on what we need to do."

"And what is that, exactly?" I watch each step we take and dodge a broken bottle on the ground.

Synn pauses and steps further into the shadows. I would have walked straight into her back if I were not paying attention. Instead, I stop just centimeters away from her and quickly glance around. Synn's hand reaches behind her back and grabs hold of my arm.

"Shhh," she quietly hisses before ducking low, pulling me down with her.

Movement over her shoulder catches my attention. There, with a baby carrier and shopping bags, is Caroline.

My kids. Do they have our children here?

Keeping as still as I can, I watch my brother's fiancée remove another bag from the back seat of a dark four-door sedan, a vehicle I do not recognize. I go to move, but Synn halts my movements.

"Don't," she whispers. "Stay low. We are to watch what she does, and once we know she is here with Leo and the twins, we move in." I nod.

Every step we continue to watch Caroline's movements, my eyes following her like a hawk. I'll make sure she pays for taking my children.

Caroline's retreating figure disappears around the corner, leaving behind the faint whisper of her footsteps. Synn pulls me along, her grip on my arm firm. We step out of the shadows, our eyes adjusting to the dim overhead lighting, and follow Caroline. Synn's whispered words, barely audible above the frantic sound of my heart thumping in my ears, break the silence as she relays Caroline's movements and their current position to her mother.

Synn stops abruptly at the corner of the building, her gaze flickering around to the other side. She glances at me over her shoulder and places her finger against her lips, signaling to remain silent and to follow her. As soon as Synn turns, she takes off for the stairs on our right. With careful steps, we make our way up the dodgy-looking staircase. My anger builds with each step. How dare Leo bring my kids here? My patience is just about gone. The steps groan under our combined weight, and I wonder if we will reach the level we need to go to.

Not sure which door the she-devil disappeared behind, we listened carefully at each door. We stop when we hear Caroline's annoying tones.

"It is your turn to change the diaper. Those smelly creatures revolt me. Hurry and get rid of the retched odor."

With raised eyebrows, Synn's eyes meet mine.

Then, the sound of a baby's cry emits the air. Relief and anger hit me at once. Finally, we've discovered the correct room. Synn lifts her finger to her lips, signifying for me to remain quiet. But, seriously, I do not know how she stays calm. I'm ready to burst into the room and shoot my brother and his fiancée.

Synn wraps her arms around me. Her lips brush my ear. "Dekk. I need you to stay here," she whispers. I shake my head in no. "Honey," she urges. "Let me handle it. When I need you to come in, I will call out. But for now, I need you to stand guard and not allow either of them to leave." With that, she gently kisses my ear before aiming for my lips.

I return her kiss with force and passion. My arms wrap around her body, holding on tight. "Please, keep safe," I manage between kisses. "Don't do anything stupid, Synn."

Essy steps away and winks at me with a nod, removes her jacket and then the gun holster. What is she doing? She slips one gun from the holster, placing it at her back in the waist of her pants and then shrugging back into her leather jacket. "Here. You need to look after the harness and my other gun."

I shake my head. Is she crazy?

Before I can think rationally, my fingers wrap around the handle of her gun. The bite of the weighted, cold, hard rubber and steel feels like they are burning my flesh. I remind myself it is only my brain playing tricks on me, my subconscious warning me — of dangerous weapons — and making sure the safety is switched on.

Synn presses her lips to mine once more and then gently encourages me to stand away from the door and out of sight.

She mutters something in her tiny mic, advising the others that she is about to go in. I see her cringe and wonder if her mother is yelling at her. Instead, she reaches for the door handle. With a quick flick of her hand and wrist, the door bursts open, and she walks in, closing the door behind her.

My brother's voice can be heard over the top of Caroline's yelling.

Shit... panic fills me when I hear my children cry.

Chapter Forty-Three

ESSY

earing their cries, my body responds automatically. My breasts ache, milk flooding my bra like a busted pipe.

Great. Just what I needed. Note to self: a kickass woman should not be seen in a soggy, milk-laden top.

Nah. On second thought, my boys come first, and anyone who thinks differently can kiss my ass.

I step into the room, chin high, eyes scanning the shadows for danger. Leo and his girlfriend freeze, their eyes wide with surprise. My gaze locks on Leo's, a silent argument sparking between us. His Adam's apple bobs as he swallows hard. He knows he's in trouble. Then I shift my focus to Caroline. Her stare is sharp, unhinged — crazyville written all over her face.

That is not a good sign.

My gaze sweeps the room again, confirming we're the only three adults here. Then I zero in on my crying babies. Relief floods me when I see them strapped into their car seats. Safe for now.

Caroline hisses something about me being in the room. Leo snaps back, telling her to shut it.

I don't see weapons, but that doesn't mean a damn thing. I move straight to my children. "Hello, my gorgeous boys. Momma missed you," I coo, voice soft even as rage simmers under my skin.

I scoop Byron up. My hand cups his diaper-covered bottom, and instantly I feel it — soaked through.

My anger spikes. My boy is wet and hungry. How incompetent are these two idiots?

"Sweets..." Leo starts.

"Don't say a word, Leo," I growl, venom dripping from every syllable.

I spot the diaper bag and move to the bed. "Hang on, little man, you'll be dry in a minute," I murmur, stripping him down, wiping him clean, and dressing him in fresh clothes. Byron calms, tears fading into a gurgling smile. My heart clenches, but my fury doesn't ease.

I glance at Leo. He's silenced Caroline, forcing her into a chair. Smart move, but too little, too late.

"Leo, hold Byron while I change Fraser," I order, voice clipped.

Even with Byron in my arms, my anger doesn't fade. Fraser is next — wet, hungry, blotchy-faced, hiccupping through tears. "What the hell have you been doing, Leo? Both boys are wet, hungry, and miserable." I change him quickly, soothing him until his sobs taper off.

I set myself up on the bed, pillows braced, breasts freed from their confines. Fraser latches instantly. I lift my hand, signaling Leo to bring Byron. He hesitates, eyes wide, then finally hands him over. Both boys feed, their tiny hands pressing against me, their gulps loud in the quiet room.

Leo sits at the end of the bed, staring. "Sweets, how do you do that? You look so beautiful feeding the boys."

I roll my eyes. "Leo, why did you take my sons?"

He meets my gaze. "One of them is mine, Sweets."

How thick is this idiot? I breathe deep, forcing calm. "No, Leo. Both boys belong to my husband. Declyn is their father. I have medical proof."

He shakes his head. "Sweets, one of the boys is my son."

I glance at Caroline. She's twitching, eyes darting, plotting something. Crazyville is winding up for a show.

"Leo, why did you take them?" My voice is steel. "Once I know my boys are safe, all bets are off."

My mother's voice whispers in my ear. "Everyone is in place. How long until we move in?"

Great. She wants a timetable.

"Leo, once the boys finish feeding, we'll talk," I say, hoping my mother hears the signal.

"Roger that. You have ten minutes," she replies.

I look down at my boys. Their eyes are wide, trusting. "Don't worry. Daddy will be here soon, and we'll go home," I whisper. Fraser kicks at the word "Daddy," recognition sparking in his little body.

Leo's voice hardens. "The boys aren't going anywhere, Sweets. Especially not back to my brother."

I meet his glare. "Don't be stupid, Leo. Dekk is their father. Not you."

"Of course you'd say that. He's your husband."

"Leo, I can honestly say Dekk is the father because I have the medical proof."

The boys drift to sleep. I gently detach them, tuck myself back into my bra. Of course, Leo is staring at my chest. Typical.

"Close your mouth, Leo. You're drooling," I mutter.

"Two minutes, Essy," my mother whispers.

"Okay," I reply. Louder, I say, "It's time to put these little guys back in their carriers."

I strap Byron in, Leo hovering too close. "Sweets, we could be good together," he whispers. "We can leave now. Take the boys and go."

Is he serious? I shake my head, secure Fraser, and place both carriers behind the bed, away from Caroline.

My mother's voice cuts in. "Door's about to open."

Time's up. It's showtime.

My hand slips to my back, under my jacket, and I draw my handgun, the weight familiar, steadying.

"Sweets," Leo says, his voice tinged with concern, "what are you doing?"

Before I can answer, the door to the room bangs open, slamming against the wall with a crash that makes the babies cry louder. The sudden noise jolts Caroline into action. She whirls, her face twisted into a snarl, and raises a gun toward me.

I don't hesitate. My weapon is already in my hand. I fire, the blast deafening, the recoil jolting up my arm. Her shot goes off almost at the same time — the sound of multiple gunshots tearing through the room, overlapping in chaos.

In slow motion, I watch Caroline's expression shift

from fury to shock. Her eyes widen, her lips part, and she glances down at the dark bloom spreading across her chest. She looks back at me, disbelief etched across her face, before her knees buckle. She crashes to the floor with a thud that shakes the air.

"Nice try, sweetheart," I mutter under my breath. "But no one points a gun at me and lives to brag about it."

I lower my weapon, steady, unflinching. "That's what happens when you threaten my children."

Then it hits me — Leo. Leo is not here.

I whip my head to the left, scanning the room. My stomach drops when I see the body near my feet, crumpled, too still. For a heartbeat I don't understand how he got there. He wasn't standing that close before.

The cry of a baby cuts through the ringing in my ears, pulling me back to reality and forcing my senses to sharpen. I look at my babies. All my mind understands is that if they're crying, they're alive. Then Leo fills my thoughts. My breath catches, sharp and ragged, as I fall to my knees beside him.

I lean over the hunched form, my hands shaking as I roll him over.

Shit. Leo. Blood everywhere. He's been shot.

And then the delayed realization slams into me — he moved. He must have lunged, shifted into my line, put himself between me and Caroline's gun. I didn't see it in the chaos, but now it's obvious. He took the bullet meant for me.

"Leo! Leo, can you hear me?" My voice is sharp, commanding, but inside I'm cursing him six ways to

Sunday. My bloodied hand presses hard against the wound, sticky warmth seeping through my fingers. He had to go and play hero. "We need a medic here!" I shout, louder, forcing control into the chaos.

The gunfire still echoes in my ears when movement at the doorway jolts me. A blur of speed and fury cuts through the chaos — Declyn. My husband rushes into the room, and for a split second my breath catches. He's here.

The sight of him slams into me harder than the recoil of my weapon. His presence is sharp, commanding, impossible to miss. My focus wavers from Leo's bloodied body just long enough to register the way Declyn moves — like a blade through air, swift, precise, dangerous.

But his first instinct isn't me, or even his brother. It's the boys. Our sons. He drops low, crouching beside their carriers, his hands steady even though his jaw is tight enough to crack. He checks them with meticulous care, scanning tiny fingers, tear-streaked faces, the rise and fall of their chests. He coos softly, his voice a low murmur meant only for them.

"Hey, little heroes," he whispers, brushing Fraser's damp hair back. "Daddy's here. You're safe now." Byron hiccups, and Declyn leans closer, soothing him with a quiet, "No more tears, champ. I've got you."

Their cries taper into whimpers, calmed by his voice. Only once he's satisfied they're safe does he haul the carriers close, anchoring them within reach. Then, and only then, does his gaze shift — locking on his brother sprawled on the floor, blood pooling beneath him.

Declyn is frozen, his eyes wide, his breath ragged. "Is he dead?" he demands. He reaches toward Leo, fingers trembling, but stops short — hovering inches above the blood-soaked shirt, as if touching him might shatter the fragile thread of life still holding. His jaw clenches, his whole body taut with shock, torn between fear and duty.

"Is he dead, Essy?" he asks, sharper this time, desperation bleeding through every syllable.

I lift one bloodied hand, sticky and trembling, and press my fingers to Leo's neck. The warmth of his blood coats my skin as I hunt for a pulse that plays hide-and-seek. Seconds stretch into eternity, each one heavier than the last. My stomach twists, bile rising, and finally I breathe out, the words tasting bitter.

"I don't know." My gaze flicks to Declyn, then back to Leo. "He stood in front of me. Leo saved me. The idiot actually saved me."

My mother's voice murmurs in my ear, calm and clinical, like she's narrating a crime scene. "Paramedics are at the door. Police two minutes out."

I repeat her words automatically, my voice hollow. Declyn doesn't move. His stare is welded to Leo, unblinking, like if he looks hard enough he can force his brother back to life.

The paramedics flood the room. One peels Declyn away with a firm hand to the shoulder; another angles toward me. "Ma'am, are you injured?"

"I don't think so," I say, still holding pressure. "He's the one shot."

"Copy. We've got him." Hands replace mine; gauze, IV, more gauze, quick clipped commands fill the air. The babies quiet, like they know the room has shifted from chaos to triage.

"Essy!" My sister's voice cuts through the ringing in my ears, and then her arms are around me, grounding me in a way I refuse to admit I need. "We heard gunshots."

"Leo is shot," I say, throat tight. "The idiot... he saved me."

She meets my eyes, steady. "It's going to be okay. Come on."

I move on autopilot. I don't remember exiting the room or traveling down the staircase — my body just keeps going, driven by instinct. Somehow I keep moving, because my boys need me. My husband will need me too. That was his twin who was shot, and the thought of Declyn hurting, knowing his brother might die — if he isn't already — twists inside me. All I know is this: now is not the place to fall apart.

We slip out behind the medics, past uniforms and questions, straight to the van. My sons blink up at me, safe, and the only thing that matters is that we're leaving. Declyn climbs in after us, rage banked but burning.

Behind us, sirens swell. Ahead of us, home waits. And if anyone wants to try taking my boys again, they can meet the same ending Caroline did.

Chapter Forty-Four

DEKK

I keep visiting my twin brother's grave, three years on. Every time I sit here, I talk to him like he's still listening. I tell him about my kids, my latest business venture, our half-brother, cousin, our mysterious grandfather, and my gorgeous wife, Synn.

"We've missed so much with Grandfather, thanks to Dad and his betrayal," I say, shaking my head. "Grandfather keeps amazing me. Last week, we had a huge family gathering. Our family is bigger than we ever imagined." Father really did a number on us, keeping us away from Grandfather and the rest of the family. All for his own greed and ridiculous revenge.

"Leo, I thank you again, my brother. For saving my wife from that bullet. You're a hero." My fingers brush along the granite headstone. His smiling face beams up at me from the picture in the center, his name, date of birth, and death carved beneath it.

One small mercy before he passed — we spoke one last time. The damn fool. Always a sucker for a beautiful woman. The night he took my twin sons, I could have killed him myself. Caroline manipulated him, convinced him my boys were his. She believed they were her babies, that Synn was her surrogate. Caroline had lost the plot. If Synn hadn't fatally shot her that night, I don't know what the crazed woman would have done. Instead, she killed my brother — the man she swore she loved.

If it weren't for Synn, I wouldn't have survived these past few years. She's been my rock, confidant, business partner, friend, lover, and gorgeous, supportive wife. What began as an arrangement — a convenient marriage — has become my salvation. Why she said yes, I'll never know. But thank the universe she did.

Every time I look at her, my heart bursts with love. I love her with all my heart and soul.

The little angel in my arms squirms again, her tiny body wriggling with determination. She makes a series of funny noises — squeaks, gurgles, and a little grunt — the unmistakable soundtrack of a baby filling her diaper. I wrinkle my nose, shaking my head. "Oh, brilliant. My daughter sounds like a squeaky toy crossed with a motorbike engine. And I know exactly what that means."

For a moment, the heaviness of talking to Leo lifts. Her gorgeous little, but deadly noises cut through the grief like sunlight breaking cloud, reminding me that life keeps moving, even when loss tries to hold me still. I can't help but smile, even here.

"So, as you can see, Leo, your niece is hungry and desperately requires a diaper change." I press my lips to

Bella's head of fine dark hair. "I miss you, brother. I hope you've found peace."

My little girl stares up at me, wide-eyed. "Say goodbye to your Uncle Leo, Bella."

She gurgles again, kicks her legs, and turns her head as if she understands. It's more like the contents of her diaper have shifted, and she doesn't like sitting in it.

"Bye, Leo. Until next time." I turn and begin walking back toward the car.

Lost in thought, I almost miss Synn's voice. "How is Leo today?" she asks from beside the car. "What did he think of his niece?"

I glance up and smile. "Look, Bella. Momma is here. She's saved me from changing you."

Synn laughs. "Dekk, you're still changing her. Then it's time to feed her."

Bugger. I was hoping to dodge this diaper. From the smell, my stomach won't appreciate it. I kiss Synn's lips before ducking down to place Bella on the change mat in the back seat. My wife has everything ready — wipes, fresh diaper, mat — all laid out like a battlefield kit.

It doesn't take long to unclip the press studs on Bella's jumpsuit and free her energetic little legs. The stench hits me like a punch to the gut. My eyes water, my throat tightens, and I gag hard.

"Oh, geez, Bella. This is chemical warfare. What has Momma been eating to cause this mess?" I cough again, fighting the acid rising in my throat.

I grip her ankles with one hand, keeping her bottom elevated above the vile excretions, sliding the toxic diaper out from under her.

"Here, Dekk, place the diaper in the plastic bag," Synn says, calm and practical.

I drop the weighted disaster into the bag, drag in a rushed breath, and mutter, "That thing should be classified as hazardous waste."

I clean Bella's delicate skin quickly, wiping her dry, then give my hands a once-over with the wipes before tossing them into the bag.

"Dekk, here, I have the new diaper ready." She passes it to me from the seat, and I slide it under Bella, sealing the tabs tight. We battle again as I wrangle her legs back into the jumpsuit.

"Bella, be good for Daddy. The quicker we get you dressed, the faster you can feed."

She pauses, gurgles, kicks her legs, then plops them down. Cheeky little imp.

I blow raspberries on her belly, making her giggle, then secure the snaps.

When I glance up, Synn is waiting in the front seat, smiling, beautiful as ever.

"Come on, you two, I'm waiting," she says, trying for a gruff voice but failing.

"Come on, Ms. Bella," I say, cuddling her once more before passing her over. "Momma's ready for you, little one. Don't forget to say, I love you, Momma."

Bella gurgles, kicking her legs, eager for her feed. Synn places her at her breast, and Bella latches on, suckling. I never tire of watching my kids drink from their mother.

Synn smiles at Bella, kisses her head, then meets my eyes. "I love you both. Always remember that."

I lean forward, brush my lips against hers. "I will always love you. You are the love of my life. My friend, lover, wife, and the mother of our children." I kiss her again, slow and passionate. "Every day, I thank my lucky stars. You became the bodyguard of my heart."

And as Bella feeds, her tiny fingers curling against Synn's skin, I feel the ache of loss twist inside me. Leo should be here. He should know his niece, tease me about gagging over diapers, laugh at her cheeky grin. He should see his nephews too — my twin boys, growing stronger every day, full of mischief and life. Instead, I sit with the memory of his sacrifice. My brother gave his life to save my wife, and because of that, I still have this moment — this family, this love.

Grief and gratitude live side by side in me. I miss him, my twin, every day, but I hold my children tighter because of him.

In the quiet of my thoughts, I whisper to him again: You'd laugh at this, you would have run from that diaper, brother.

Chapter Forty-Five

ESSY

FIVE YEARS LATER.

"*L*aini, time's up," I call out through the closed bathroom door. "What's the result?" My foot taps against my granite-tiled floor. My patience has worn thin.

For the last week, she had suspected she might be pregnant. Then, this morning Laini asked to use my bathroom because she did not want to try the test at her place when her husband worked from home. So, with two pregnancy tests in her hand, she casually walked into my bathroom.

I have gone past my time-waiting threshold.

"Come on, Laini. What does the test say?"

"Shit… it's saying I'm pregnant, Essy," Laini's voice rising to a squeak. "How in the world can I be pregnant at my age?"

Well, I will not mention that plenty of women are becoming pregnant at our age. Plus, not being on birth, control can do it.

"Maybe don't have unprotected sex," I mumble under my breath. I step closer to the bathroom. "Open the bloody door, Laini. Give me a look at the stupid test. Did you remember to use the second test as a backup?"

The door opens wide, and I take a step back. Laini appears, holding two pregnancy tests in her hand. Her hair is messed up, as if she had constantly been running her fingers through it many times.

"Yeah. Yeah. Of course, I used both of them. They say the same thing." Laini looks up from the test. "I'm pregnant!"

Oh, my. The reality of seeing them makes it real.

OMG. My sister is pregnant after all these years, and I smile.

"Wow. How do you feel about it?"

She smiles, then frowns. "I'm not sure. Don't get me wrong. This is an exciting time. But am I ready?"

I wrap my arms around her shoulders and squeeze tight. "Yes, Laini, you are ready. You have been ready for a long time. Now, you can go through the pregnancy with your husband by your side."

Laini married her long-time love, who is also the father of their thirteen-year-old daughter. Nearly fourteen years ago, he had married another woman, never knowing Laini was pregnant. Back then, his parents, not accepting Laini, who was seventeen, organized an arranged marriage for their only son.

After all those years apart, Laini and Jaxton have a second chance at life and love.

"What am I going to tell Jax?"

"What you should have said to him fourteen years ago."

"Essy, don't be a bitch." Oooo. Touchy. I only wish I had known about her teenage pregnancy. I could have been there for her.

"I was honest, Laini. It's time for the two of you to grab life and enjoy it. Now you have a new baby to enjoy."

"But…"

"No, buts. Go make an appointment with your doctor and have the pregnancy confirmed. Then surprise your husband with the news." My eyebrows move up and down as I smile.

Her worried frown turns into a smiling face of excitement. But then, it might be how Laini thinks of her husband. Several years ago, Laini and Jaxton surprised us with a dinner party. We thought it was to announce they were getting married. Instead, the dinner party was to celebrate their first wedding anniversary. Our parents were not impressed with another daughter getting hitched without them being there to witness the ceremony.

Even after all this time, Laini and Jaxton still act like a pair of teenagers in love.

"Okay, Essy."

I watch my fun-loving sister go to her handbag and remove her cell.

Right. Time to give her some privacy.

*T*tap my fingers against the cup of tea sitting between my hands. The second steaming brew on my kitchen table slowly cools. That's it. I lean forward and place my cup down on the tabletop. My patience is wearing thin as I wait for Laini to enter the kitchen.

Geez, how long does it take to make an appointment?

Light footsteps echo along the tiled hallway behind me — Laini.

I shift my laptop and paperwork to the side and concentrate on Laini as she sits opposite me.

She reaches for a chocolate biscuit from the plate on the table. She dunks it in her cup and quickly sucks the melting chocolate between her lips before eating it.

I shake my head at her antics. But unfortunately, my adorable sister has never changed that habit. She still ate chocolate biscuits the same way since we were teenagers.

My eyebrow raises, waiting for her to fill me in on her phone call.

She smiles at me. Her lips and teeth are coated in chocolate.

What is she... five?

"Seriously, Laini. Lick your lips or something. You have chocolate covering your mouth."

All it would take is for one of my kids to see her act

this way, and they, too, will think they can behave in such a manner.

After a few sips of her hot drink and quickly running her tongue over her lips and teeth, it does not take long to clear all traces of chocolate from her mouth.

"All better?" she asks with a smile. Then, instead of mentioning her appointment, she takes another mouthful of tea.

"Laini... Are you going to inform me of your phone call? Did you make an appointment?"

She nods as her facial features turn serious. "Yes. My doctor wants to perform a sonogram while I am there." Really? How far is the pregnancy? "Can you go with me? It's in an hour."

Shit. By the looks of Laini's face, she's concerned something might be wrong.

"Yes. I'll be there. So, do you need to drink a liter of water before we go?" I remember when I had my scans, I had to drink gallons of the stuff. Not comfortable at all. All I wanted to do was pee myself.

She nods before taking another mouthful of tea, then grabs another biscuit.

After selecting water bottles from the pantry, I pass them to her. "Here. These will come in handy."

*L*ess than two hours later, we stare at the dark screen containing a white blob in the shape of a baby. We listen to the fast, whooshing beat of Laini's baby's heart echoing around the room. I glance at her face containing a huge smile that reaches from ear to ear. Her eyes match mine, full of happy tears.

"Congratulations, Sis," is all I can manage. I still cannot believe she has gone four months without realizing she's pregnant. Four months! Well, eighteen weeks, but seriously... how did she not know?

The doctor's voice echoes in the small room, and I just about jump. "As you can see, the heart is healthy and strong. Your baby is progressing finely, and all his toes and fingers can be seen. The spine is fully formed. Before you leave, I want to take blood from you to ensure everything is fine. You know, standards tests."

I stop watching the screen and turn toward the doctor. "What are you not telling us?" He glances my way before looking back toward Laini.

"Mrs. Travelli, I know this is not your first pregnancy. But, at your age, we need to take some extra precautions. Plus, take pregnancy vitamins."

Laini nods. I can see she is becoming agitated. "Doctor, I have been taking women's multivitamins for several months now because I feel drained and tired. It turns out I was pregnant! How did the doctor I'd seen at my last medical appointment miss the symptoms?"

Yes. How did the doctor not notice? When she arrived at my place after her appointment, she looked like death warmed up and had fallen asleep on my lounge. I had never seen her in that condition before. While she slept, I purchased some multivitamins at the local drugstore. Thankfully, I had convinced Laini to try the vitamin pills.

I faced the doctor again and requested, "Doctor, Laini would like a couple of pictures of the baby to show her husband. He would have been here instead of me if he had known she was pregnant this morning."

He nods his head and prints out several pictures.

*L*aini pulls up outside my apartment building in the drop-off zone. "Thanks for going with me, Essy."

"Where else would I be, Laini? You're my sister. I'll always be there for you." And I would. She has always been there for me. I don't know how I can repay her. "Now, go and speak with your husband. I bet he will be shocked but thrilled at becoming a parent again. Then, if you want, I can mind my gorgeous niece and give the two of you some adult time together," I say, and wiggle my eyebrows suggestively.

Laini laughs. "Yeah, that's just the thing. That is what got us in this predicament in the first place."

I begin to laugh. "At least you cannot get any more pregnant."

"True. Very true." Laini leans over the middle console and hugs me. "Thanks again, and yes, I think we will take you up on the babysitting. Can you meet Emma at the school pickup?"

"Yes. What else is super fun, aunties, for?" I say with a laugh and pull away. I love spending time with my niece, making up for all those early years I missed in her life.

"Thanks, Sis. Remember — I love you. Now, I better go home, make dinner arrangements, and shower. I can still feel the sticky gel on my skin," she says with an over-the-top shudder.

I open the car door and stand. "Love you, too. Don't forget. We have spare clothes and stuff here for Emma, so we don't need to return to your place. Have fun and enjoy."

With a smile, Laini says, "I will. But this time, everything will be different. I finally have the man I love, and our family is back together. Now go. I have stuff to do and little time to do it."

As she drives off, another laugh escapes me. I bet Laini and Jaxton don't even leave their house tonight!

THANK YOU

Thank you for reading The Bodyguard's Convenient Marriage, my second contemporary novella. I hope you enjoyed it as much as I loved writing about Essy and Dekk.

After reading, consider leaving and writing a review, even if it is a few words like 'I loved this book' or 'I enjoyed it! It kept me turning the page.'

It will assist other readers in selecting their next book. You help keep me in work by reading this book, so pass the word and tell your friends to grab a copy.

If you would like to learn more about what I am writing or competitions, sign up for my newsletter. https://mltompsett.com/newsletter-signup/

If you're interested in reading one of my other books, check me out on my website, Bookbub, or Goodreads, to name a few places.

www.mltompsett.com

ACKNOWLEDGMENTS

To my special people who I hound and annoy with my writings — you know who you are, especially Ange, thank you from the bottom of my heart. Your advice, idea's, and comments have been invaluable, big hugs guys. Without you, my book would not be finished.

As always, thank you, to my boys—big hugs.

THANK YOU
AND
HAPPY
READING

The Bodyguard's Convenient Marriage

www.ingramcontent.com/pod-product-compliance
Lightning Source LLC
Chambersburg PA
CBHW020347120726
47904CB00002B/482